MW00834428

THE ZOOKEEPER

THE ZOOKEEPER

AMMARAH REHMAN

MANUSCRIPTS PRESS

COPYRIGHT © 2023 AMMARAH REHMAN
All rights reserved.

THE ZOOKEEPER

ISBN

979-8-88926-500-9 *Paperback*
979-8-88926-501-6 *Ebook*

for Mama, Papa, and my two older brothers,
Jahangir and Saife

CONTENTS

"One hand, five homes. A lifetime in a fist"

—JHUMPA LAHIRI, THE NAMESAKE

AUTHOR'S NOTE

———

During the holy month of Ramzan, households all around Pakistan watch a tear-jerking, heart-wrenching commercial from Shan Masala, a renowned spice brand. In the summer of 2015, I watched this advertisement with my cousins during my visit to Karachi, Pakistan.

It marked my first experience fasting in a Muslim-majority country. The entire country transforms during the holy month of Ramzan, similar to the way every street corner is decorated with shimmering lights, homes embellished with trees, and malls and stores that play Christmas music during the holiday season in the United States.

Ramzan is a time of fervent devotion and prayer. People fast for thirty days—refraining from food, water, and other human pleasures—from the crack of dawn until sunset. The entire city stirs before sunrise to nibble on food before the sirens blare, signaling the time to stop eating. It was my first time religiously waking up before the call to prayer that echoed throughout the streets.

The evening meal, known as iftar, is a vibrant celebration. Plates were laden with samosas, spicy chickpeas, tangy tamarind sauce, and greasy fried dough with onions. My family eagerly piled our plates high, awaiting the evening call to prayer that granted us permission to relish our food.

Huddled close together, my cousins waited for the countdown to begin. With the TV in front of us, we sat with our food on our plates and our palms out in front of us to pray before the meal. All the while, the local news channels aired special programs, commercials, and the countdown to break the fast. Amid the shows, the TV ran the famous Shan Masala advertisement.

Two brothers appear on a rooftop in a place that looks like the United States yet is ambiguous enough to be any Western country. The younger brother, sobbing, says to his older brother, "This doesn't feel like Ramzan," implying how they are without their family members and unable to follow the traditions of Ramzan. The older brother snuggles his younger brother and rubs his head affectionately.

The next scene cuts to the older brother roaming the streets looking for something until he stumbles upon a Pakistani grocery store. He walks through the aisles and finds the Shan Masala spices. He grabs a few spice boxes and heads home. Next thing you know, onions and peppers are tossed into a pan with a huge smile on his face. While the food cooks, he decorates the house with lights. He arranges the table—biryani, spicy chickpeas, samosas, chicken rolls—the same display in front of me as I watch the commercial.

The younger brother returns home with a gloomy face. As he enters the house, the aroma of the food strikes him. Immediately he cries out, "Mother?" Thinking his mother might be inside. Searching for his mother, he finds instead his brother waiting for him to share a meal that reminds them of home.

When the commercial ends, my cousin's eyes swell. She looks at me and says, "This is how your father must feel every Ramzan without us, his family."

The thought never occurred to me how my father must feel thousands of miles away from his family in the United States, eating meals with a fork and spoon. It would be like celebrating Christmas without any family. There are no calls to pray in the United States, no alarms, or men walking around with drums to wake you up in the morning. He sacrificed being able to enjoy the traditions of his hometown to provide for his family back home.

My cousin is probably right. My father probably does sneak away to shed a few tears every Ramzan while remembering the taste of his mother's home-cooked meals. I remember the stories his friends and he told us about first moving to the United States. How different things felt, even the most obvious things didn't make sense to them. They would tell stories about what troubles they would get into as young men living away from home for the first time in their twenties.

The Zookeeper is a tale about Jahangir, a young man tasked to bring animals to the United States. When he arrives, his animals go missing, and he searches for them while living with other Pakistani men, surviving in the United States and trying to make a living.

This novel is mainly fiction but is based on the stories I heard my father and his friends tell us about first moving to the United States.

I do not have any prior writing experience; I have never written a story, let alone a novel. I often read novels written by Pakistani Americans about a different perspective of the American dream that never resonated with me. My experience was different. My father came to the United States and worked in parking lots, gas stations, and convenience stores. Where was his story of struggle and survival?

Driven to bring these untold narratives to light, I wrote this book. My book serves as a testament to individuals who leave their hometowns in pursuit of a better life. The men in our families labored over a hundred hours a week as taxi drivers, cashiers at stores, and grueling all-night shifts at parking lots. Their efforts were worthwhile as they worked for a better future for their parents and siblings.

This book is for anyone who has immigrated to another country and worked endlessly to support their loved ones. This book is for the Babas and Papas who work tirelessly to support their families back in their motherland. This book is for anyone with a parent who was the breadwinner of their family. This book is an immigrant survival story for the entire immigrant community worldwide.

This book is for me. This book is for Papa.

I pray the homeland becomes so rich

That no mother, sister, daughter, or wife

Has to exchange dollars, euros, or pounds

For rupees, fathers, brothers, sons, or husbands.

CHAPTER 1

NAZIMABAD

───

March 12, 1988

Parrots are the only animals in the world to talk like humans. They mimic our words without knowing what they are saying. High-pitched sounds flow from the curled tips of their beaks like an enchanted song. But their mimicry lacks true communication with us; it remains an impossible feat.

They are trying to adapt to us. I can't explain the science behind it, but I've heard the parrots mimic other animal noises too. Parrots are social animals like us, adjusting to the environment, possibly a survival mechanism used in the wild. Perhaps by sounding like animals in their habitat, they are safer and no longer a threat. Humans are culprits to this phenomenon too.

As I prepare to feed the animals at Al-Ahmed Animal House, I look around as though looking for the very first time. Within the tranquil expanse of nearly ten acres, the sanctuary's humble space allows zebras to frolic freely while pomegranate trees spread their roots, gracing me with their bountiful fruits. The mingling aromas of fresh cow manure and blooming gardenias fill the air.

In the early hours, before any of my fellow workers arrive, I find solace in observing the parrots. The morning sun peers through their metal enclosures, casting a rhythmic pattern of parallel lines upon the ground. Its warm rays embrace the parrots, illuminating their vivid plumage painted in shades of crimson, turquoise, and gold. The parrots' songs flood my ears. The sounds elicit a calming, almost meditative state in me.

Before I can drift too far away, Aziz nudges me, bringing me back into the present. The harsh break of my daze brings me back into reality. We have to complete our morning tasks.

"Grab the blue plastic buckets on the floor, Jahangir bhai," he says, pointing at the bucket. Aziz still refers to me as bhai even after I told him he doesn't have to be so formal. He's new here, a young man with a thick mustache gracing his face, and his skin is sun-kissed from working outside. He'll loosen up soon enough and start calling me all sorts of names.

I grab the buckets. Aziz and I wheel cumbersome sacks of bird feed filled with pellets, smelling of hay and barley, over to the parakeet cages by the banyan trees.

The morning is feeding time here in Al-Ahmed Animal House. The animals can't feed themselves—a life of luxury they live here.

The parrots don't have to worry about surviving or defending themselves against predators. Those obligations fall on me. Being a voice for the voiceless is a zookeeper's job. The animals don't hunt for their next meal. We are the hunters, supplying them with their next kill. Sometimes we are the animals' voice of reason. We have to observe their body language to understand whether they are sick. How fast or slow they approach us will let us know what they want from us.

"Food! Food! Food," the gray parrot says as Aziz approaches the cage. The other birds screech and sing in different tones, all eager and impatient for their food, like wailing babies waiting to be fed. They latch onto the cage with their nimble beaks.

"How do parrots even know how to talk like us?" Aziz ponders as he lifts the cage door to pour feed into the plastic cup.

"How does it speak Urdu?" he asks, confused. "Does the bird even know it's talking to us? Every time I walk over to the cage and say it's time to eat, the parrot repeats after me and knows it's time to eat," Aziz says while measuring the feed into the navy-blue buckets.

"You know those parrots also cry like the kids who visit this place," I recall. "I was walking around the bird cages during visiting hours the other day, and I heard a kid crying. I was worried someone left their child behind." I write the date and time on the clipboard to track the feeding schedule. "I looked around the path to see where the child was and saw no one. I thought it was a jinn, but then I heard the sound coming from the cage again." I point to the cage it was coming from.

Aziz laughs hysterically. "I would run if I didn't find a child. I don't want to see a jinn here."

"I know there aren't any here. Salim bhai is a religious man, and jinns aren't on land owned by people like him," I say with a grunt as I stack one last sack of bird feed onto the rusty wheelbarrow.

Salim bhai runs a lucrative business out of Nazimabad, importing and exporting some of the most beautiful birds and animals. Macaws with rainbows hidden under their wings, toucans with bright marmalade beaks, white cockatoos with marigold feathers sticking up on top of their heads, and hundreds of parakeets chirp all day.

Looking around at the cages, I ask, "Where did you start feeding this morning, Aziz?"

"I started in section one by the tamarind trees," he calls out while rolling the wheelbarrow and heading to the next section of hungry birds.

Aziz and I unload the sacks of bird feed. I toss bags over my shoulder and onto the ground, causing a loud thudding sound. He pulls out a small knife from his cotton trousers and tears through the sack at the top. Bird seed pours out onto the ground, and Aziz scoops up the feed to measure precisely against the marked line on the navy-blue buckets.

We take turns filling up all the animal cages with their appropriate diet. We scoop a bunch of feed from sacks to buckets and then pour out the seeds in the feeders aligned in the cell. We repeat these motions several dozen times, creating a rhythm and soothing sound from the pellets hitting the buckets. The sound of the pellets hitting the metal alerts the animals that it is time to eat. We repeat these motions, moving from one cage to another.

As I watch Aziz taking another scoop, I cannot help but feel a sense of duty towards him. I remember when I first started here, knowing full well there are several things that I have yet to teach him.

I again gaze out at the sprawling expanse of Al-Ahmed Animal House, but this time, I feel a mix of awe and unease. This sanctuary is a place where animals are bred, nurtured, and eventually sold to other zoos across the globe—a fact that leaves a bitter taste in my mouth.

As I walk through the bird section, I marvel at the care each animal is given. We breed them to be strong and live long lives. We feed, bathe, and clean them for visitors to observe before shipping them around the world to their next destination.

Despite the beauty I am surrounded by, I can't shake off the knowledge that these animals are destined for a life in captivity. Sold to zoos in Japan, Turkey, and America, they spend their days behind bars.

For now, I push those thoughts aside and focus on life before me. Birds of all colors flit around in their cages with their wings a blur of motion as they sing. In a nearby enclosure, lion cubs chase after each other, their soft roars filling the air. Baby chimps snuggle against their mothers' breasts.

As I move about the sanctuary, sweat collects on my forehead and slowly rolls down my face and neck. I pick up buckets of feed and pour seeds and nuts into the feeders in the cages.

We mainly tend to male birds since they are the attractive ones. It is their job to lure in the females with their beguiling feathers. Only the most precious singers will win the affection of the females. The African gray parrots mate for life, a bond stronger than some of us humans who are never satisfied with just one mate.

Reaching into the cage of the lime green parakeet, I can't help but smile at its flirtatious singing. The bird hops on my arm and nibbles on my fingers, which smell of seeds. I grab the feathers at the bottom of the cage and wipe away any dirt or waste.

The owner keeps one gray parrot as their pet and refuses to sell it. Salim bhai is particularly interested in the gray parrot and how it can mimic words of the *azan*, the call to prayer. He refused to sell the parrot that repeated the words of Allah, claiming Allah shows us his existence through these animals, keeping them afloat through the sky with ease. If there wasn't a God, how could such a miracle as flight happen?

"I always want to leave the cages open. You deserve to fly and spread those beautiful wings," I say under my breath as I pet the parakeet on its head. The bird scrunches its head, causing its feathers to ruffle closer to its face.

"She is really fond of you," Aziz says while sliding the tray at the bottom of the cage.

"I hand-fed her when she was first born here. We must carefully and delicately feed the newborns by hand and raise them in those glass incubators for several months. We coddle them just like babies," I say, looking at the bird smashing the seeds.

"Except we don't keep our children in cages like we keep these birds. Animals weren't meant to be in cages the way we've locked them away," I tell Aziz.

"When I first started working here, I was a child," I say. "I had fragile hands like a woman. If you'd put henna on them, they would have looked like a woman's hands. These hands were perfect for hand-feeding the baby birds." I lift one of my hands closer to my face.

"But now these hands look like they have seen a life-time-worth of labor," I say walking toward Aziz.

"They have grown and adjusted to the roughness of those sacks," I mumble, wiping them on my trousers.

"What a blessing from Allah to make us adaptable to this world. Any challenge, any circumstance, our bodies, and minds learn to adjust." I grab the water gallons and pour them out into the containers for the birds.

From a distance, I notice Salim bhai walking over to us, striding with deliberate force. The white hairs in his beard glisten. He hardly approaches us during the day unless it's something important. My stomach sinks as I watch him walk toward us, wondering what news he brings. Sensing the gravity of the situation, Aziz stands up straight and dusts off his shirt. The seeds and nuts fall on the ground, mimicking the sound of rain.

"Asalam Alaykum," Aziz and I say in unison.

"Walikum Asalam," Salim bhai says.

"Jahangir and Aziz, we have a shipment that will leave for America next Friday," Salim bhai utters.

I exchange a glance with Aziz, who shrugs. Why is this so important as to warrant a visit from him? We have shipments that go out every Friday. My forehead scrunches, puzzled by the statement.

"We need one of you to go with the animals to America, take care of them, and ensure they make it safely."

One of us. My heart plummets into shock as Salim bhai's words pierce my ears. Fingers trembling, I cling to the ends of my shirt, desperately seeking comfort in the fabric while my restless feet shake from anticipation and unease.

Glimpsing over at Aziz, I yearn for a reassuring look. Yet his expression mirrors my own trepidation. Doubt and anxiety wage a war within me.

"The shipment will include hundreds of parakeets, a gray parrot, a markhor, and a white tiger." Salim bhai's words hang in the air, casting a surreal haze over my mind.

Why does someone need to travel with the animals? How long will the voyage last? We commonly ship birds around the globe, never requiring such a personal touch. Questions swirl within me, engulfing me in my thoughts. An acute, almost searing pain throbs within my head.

"The journey could take several months and several more to help settle the animals," Salim bhai explains. "All your living arrangements will be made when you get to the location. I need a decision by tomorrow," Salim bhai says as he walks away, vanishing behind a row of cages.

I look over at Aziz, whose eyes are wide open in disbelief.

"What are you thinking, Jahangir bhai?" Aziz asks.

The birds sing around us, but silence washes over me. Salim bhai's words echo in my mind—America. To bring animals. A chance to leave.

I don't know how to respond. I don't know what to think. Could this be my chance to escape and never come back? So many men I grew up with have left in search of a better life, just like these animals, bred and raised here only to be sold off elsewhere.

"Do you want to go?" I ask Aziz.

He shakes his head. "I just got married, and my father needs me," he replies, sighing.

"What do you think, Jahangir bhai?" he asks again.

"I am thinking we still got cages by the mangrove trees and the parakeets in the field next to pomegranate trees to feed." I evade the question, unsure what to make of Salim bhai's request.

"Visitors will arrive soon. We need to finish feeding before they arrive," I say, stacking the buckets.

America. The land where the poor turn rich. America. A place where no problems exist. As the final cage is cleaned and the last bird is fed, Aziz and I walk over to the rest house.

He stacks all the blue and white buckets back in place, and I count how many bags of seeds we used and how many more we need to order.

"Jahangir bhai, I think that's all for today," Aziz says as he gathers his belongings.

"That's it. You are doing a great job here," I reassure him, looking into his beady black eyes.

"I know you'll take care of everything here if I leave." I ruffle his hair. Just this morning I was thinking about the time we were going to spend working and learning at the sanctuary together.

I place the clipboard back on the pegs against the shelf and fill out the other forms to order more bird feed. Gathering my things, I head home early.

Salim bhai's words ring in my ears. America? Really? The place where dreams come true. America is a place where everything is possible. Many people apply for visas. One day they are on the streets of Nazimabad buying their milk in plastic bags, and the next day they are swept off to the land of hope. I remember listening on the radio about their president, an actor in Hollywood, a handsome man with a strong jawline. The newspaper mentioned he won the majority of the election votes. It was a landslide win.

I've worked here all these years to pay for my family's endeavors, only wanting the best for them. Salim bhai mentioned that the client is willing to pay double for someone to deliver the animals to him from the port. That would be enough money to buy my parents a new home.

Who will take care of my family if I make it to America? I can't bear to hurt them. I can barely swallow the thought.

As I weigh the decision to leave for America, I can't help but think about my family. Papa is growing old and deserves a better place to live. The ceiling leaks every year during the monsoon season, destroying the plaster and causing the damask wallpaper to peel. Brown circular stains mock me every morning. They prey on me, reminding me to get up, provide for my family, and give them a better life.

I need to inform my family about going to America. My responsibility as the eldest son of our house is to provide for them. They aren't my only responsibility.

Haleema's stomach grows rounder each day. Her face, feet, and breasts are swollen from the child we expect in a few months. It's hard to recognize her as the same person I married several months back.

We chose each other, unlike most of the arranged marriages that happen in Nazimabad. Our love is strong, but she won't be happy knowing about my departure. How do I bring it up? How do I explain to her that I want to give our family a better future, and this may be the only way? I would be back in just a few months, or maybe I could find a job there and move our family.

She will understand. I will convince her, just as I persuaded her to marry me.

From the moment our eyes met, I had fallen deeply in love with her. It was as if the very air had been sucked out of my lungs, replaced by her essence—the reason I existed. Carved in my memory is the day I caught sight of her gracefully walking to the grade school where she taught Urdu. Her hair, like a curtain of dark, lustrous strands, playfully escaped from beneath the scarf that adorned her head. Never before had my eyes beheld such exquisite beauty. So captivating was she that I nearly lost control of my motorcycle as I drove past her.

Over the following months, I drove by the same alleyway hoping to catch another fleeting glimpse of her. Then, one day, she was walking alone without her sister, and I decided to talk to her. I was utterly smitten. To my agony, anytime I got close to her, I felt tongue-tied when trying to speak. Days turned to months of me waiting to say a few words again.

I ached to be away from her. I longed for the smell of her mustard hair oil and wanted to gaze into her eyes, marked with the allure of black kohl.

She would warn me to stay away, that her father might catch her speaking to me. Or worse, her brother's friends might snitch on her. It was worth the risk for me. One day, I caught her name from the name tag on her shirt, Haleema. The Prophet Muhammad's foster mother's name, and a name I hoped to call out for the rest of my life. I would convince her to be my wife. Anytime I asked her hand in marriage, she would shrug me off confidently and tell me she didn't plan on marrying. "Marriage is for the weak," she would say. She wanted to teach, claiming that it was an act of resilience.

She walked around with books filled with love poems by Mirza Ghalib or Parveen Shakir. Months later, I asked her to write me a love poem. I carried her poetry books for her sometimes as I walked her to school. She would point out her favorite poems and recite them to me by heart. Her voice was as sweet as honey to my ears. My heart would tingle as the sounds of the words left her tongue. How I wanted to hold her and shower her with my love.

I spent hours trying to memorize two lines of the poems she reads to recite back to her.

She would recite her favorite poem every time I'd ask her to marry me—about love being like a river of fire. To cross the river of fire, you must be fully embodied, drowning in love.

And I was willing to drown in her river of fiery love.

I need to tell her I will drown in a different river of fire—one that leads to a different goal, with love not at the other end.

I won her over after some time. Now, I must convince her that I am leaving for a better life for us. With my family and my father growing older, this is the right decision.

I clasp onto the metal gate of my home, thinking about what I should say to Haleema.

CHAPTER 2

DHUHR

———

Nothing will be the same when I walk inside. How will everyone react to the news of my departure? Will they understand? Do I even want to leave? Asad, the local shopkeeper, went to study in America five years ago, and now his family lives like royal kings and queens. Rumors spread in our neighborhood that he married another woman to stay in America.

I eye the rusting steel gate in front of me. Its intricate design and its familiarity welcome me home. I squeeze my hand through the arch opening at the top to unlock it. I pull on the gold handle, releasing the lock with a clicking sound.

As I enter the door, I hear the call to prayer. This leaves me only a few minutes to cleanse myself. Papa always wants to be in the first row when we pray, claiming if we understood the amount of spiritual reward we receive for being in the first row, we would kill each other over those spots.

I hope he has already left for the masjid so I can get out of praying with him. Going with Papa means staying at the masjid while he completes his extra prayers. I am not one of Allah's strongest believers.

"Asalam Alaykum, Raja," Papa greets me by my childhood name.

"Hurry, my child, I don't want to be in the back," he says, ushering me toward the bathroom.

"I'm waiting by the door," he calls out as I slip on the bathroom sandals. I slide over the buckets for bathwater and twist open the faucet. Water rushes out with a strong scent of salt. The area where the water collects is grainy amber. It's rusting away. I perform my ablution in threes. I wash my face three times, my hands three times, and proceed to clean my mouth, nose, arms, hair, ears, and feet. Cold water trickles down my arms and legs, marking my readiness for prayer.

In a hurry to reach the masjid, Papa always takes three steps for every two of mine, tapping his walking stick along the way. As we arrive, we remove our shoes at the open arches of the masjid entrance, placing them securely on a wooden shelf near the bottom.

The masjid smells like the earth and flowers. A strong aroma of jasmine lingers in the air as small dry white petals collect on the turquoise tiles.

Papa limps to the first row. He hurries to a spot on the maroon Persian rugs and places his prayer beads back in his pocket.

Men slowly gather in hushed tones as shoes hit the wooden shelf, echoing throughout the masjid. As the room fills, the imam instructs us to stand closer to one another, shoulder to shoulder. He begins praying when enough men congregate inside. With our hands on our stomachs, the imam's melody of Arabic words, foreign yet memorized by my heart, reverberates through the room.

As I lose my concentration, the words float away. The decision still lies ahead of me. I know so little about the world outside of these streets, and I am limited to only my knowledge of my animals. My stomach turns, and I feel myself sweating again. Instead of praying, I am searching for the words to say to my family. They will think their oldest son is abandoning them. An unsettling sensation courses through my body, causing goosebumps to erupt and every hair on my back to stand on end.

"Allah Akbar." The imam's attentive voice brings me back to prayer. My wavering concentration causes my hands to delay when reaching for my knees, a beat slower than the other worshippers.

I rub my hands together and take several slow, deep breaths. Slowly, I focus on the words recited.

Several minutes later, the prayer ends, but I remain seated on the ground with my arms out in front of me. I hold my hand out in the air, asking for protection and guidance in the journey ahead as doubts gnaw in my head.

I blow out the prayers from my mind onto myself and open my eyes to find my father standing above me, having completed the prayer before me. He places a frail hand on my shoulder as we walk to find our shoes.

"It's a shame there weren't that many people here for prayer," Papa says as we slide our feet in our sandals.

Papa goes on about the missing members at prayer as we walk home. "Every prayer should look like the Friday prayers. Hundreds of men come to pray on Friday but only on Friday," he says as we exit the masjid.

"I'm tired of pulling the young men by their ears to attend the prayer. They keep saying they're coming and that they will join me. But when I leave the masjid, they are still playing cricket," Papa continues complaining about the boys in the neighborhood who avoid him during prayer time as we slowly walk home.

I chuckle bitterly to myself, contemplating how I've become just like those boys who run away from him.

As we approach home, the savory smell of onions and garlic frying lingers through the air. Papa lovingly strokes the soft fur of the neighborhood cats that faithfully trail behind us. A cat purrs under his gentle touch.

With a series of clicks, the metallic door swings open, and we step inside, dutifully removing our shoes and leaving them by the entrance.

"Is it you, jaan?" Haleema calls out from the kitchen, never referring to me by my name and only through words of endearment.

"Yes, I'm back," I say while walking to the kitchen. She flattens out balls of dough for roti. The sound of the rolling pin hitting the old counter echoes throughout the house.

I wash my hands and catch glances of Haleema in the kitchen, stirring the pot of lentils.

I can't help but notice her red and white spotted chunri outfit. The red complementing her ochre skin and dark silky hair. How I want to kiss her full lips. Her stomach is starting to bulge out slightly. She occasionally rests her hand on her belly as she stirs the pots. It's hard to look away from her beauty.

In the dimly lit kitchen, the concrete floor stretches out under her, and water trickles from the sink. Chipped and cracked cabinet doors swing on feeble hinges, barely clinging to their weathered frames.

Haleema's chiffon scarf is draped over one of the kitchen chairs, waiting patiently to be worn should my brother or father walk in.

Bits of flour collect on her forehead from wiping off the sweat while cooking. Her keen eyes focus on the task at hand while the pot steams. She kneads out the bread, pushing it down and then outward, using only the heels of her hands. She rests her small bump on the counter with her hand supporting her lower back. Her lips say it all without even making a noise. I know she is in discomfort. I wish I could ease her pain. Instead, I will be adding to it. Is there a way to tell her about leaving without hurting her? I wince at the thought of telling her I must leave.

Shards of glass glint in the fading light, reflecting Haleema's beauty. As her bold eyes meet her own in the distorted reflection, a tender warmth emerges in her.

"Asalam Alaykum," she says in a hushed tone, almost to herself, making sure no one else hears the intimacy in her voice.

With the thoughts running through my head, I delay responding.

"To what do I owe your early return home? Are you going to return to the animals or stay for food?" Haleema asks while peeling the dough off the counter and flipping it back and forth in her hands before placing it on the circular griddle.

"I went to pray with Papa," I say as my hand clutches the corner of the steel sink. My stomach bubbles, and I feel like I am about to vomit.

Her love for me anchors her to this house. Her only reason for living here is because she married me. As a woman, she must live in her husband's home. Will she be upset that

I am leaving her? I will be back in a few months; I might be back in time for our baby's birth. But the possibility of never returning exists if other opportunities arise.

"Listen," Haleema says while waving a hand in my face. "What's wrong? You look more lost than the animals you take care of." Haleema lets out a sly smile.

She fixes her hair and places the scarf over her head, patting her hair under it as she pushes past me to bring the food to the dining area.

The lentils are left on the stove to boil a bit longer. As the bubbles form, the lentils slowly rise in the pot.

I wait in the kitchen for her to come back. Should I tell her now or later? I will have to leave by Friday.

"Haleema, I need to talk to you," I yell as she reappears in the kitchen.

Her brows furrow. She does not notice the anticipation on my face. "Let me just put this in the dining room," Haleema says. She walks away swiftly as her scarf blows over my chest, slipping off her head.

The pot boils a bit more. The yellow lentils rise high to the surface, nearly spilling over.

Without me, she will be alone with our child if I do not return in time. Alone with my parents, burdened with the responsibility to care for them. The thoughts cloud my head, and I am unable to put my words together.

"What do you need to tell me?" Haleema asks, entering the kitchen and looking for something to wipe her hands on.

"I… I…" I choke. My heart beats in my chest.

"I have to go." I flush. My face grows hot. "I have to go to America."

The lentils spill out of the pot as soon as the words leave my mouth. Haleema ignores the stove, allowing the food to overflow and leave a grainy yellow mess on the stove. Her large black eyes stare into mine. She wasn't paying attention to me until now. She hadn't sensed the tension in my face. "America." Her voice trails off as she covers her mouth. "*Allah ki qasam?* You swear on God?" she asks, blinking her weary eyes several times.

"A new shipment needs to be hand-delivered to America, and there are a few special requests for some particular animals," I say as Haleema's intense eye contact breaks. She turns around and twists the knobs of the stove, letting out a soft tisk of disappointment seeing the lentils spilled on the stovetop.

"I have to go with the animals to take care of them since the journey is long, and we can't send them any other way other than by ship—"

"What about our child?" Haleema asks with tears swelling in her lash line. Her cheeks turn a rosy pink. "You won't be here when he is born?"

An uneasy draft fills the kitchen, and a nervous tension hangs between us. The unsaid fills the space between our bodies about whether I should go and leave my family behind. They need me here more than I think. I feel conflicted, trying to figure out what the right decision is.

"But I have to go," I reason with her. "They will pay me a lot for this trip. More money than I've made over the years. We might be able to have our own zoo one day if this goes well," I plead with her. "Then I can send people to America with our birds and animals just like Salim bhai."

Haleema sighs and shakes her head. She is not convinced.

"No one ever returns from there," she says as tears drip from her eyes.

I caress her stomach. The palm of my hand rests on the indent from her belly button. With my other hand, I stroke her hair. Tears trickle down her face. I am in agony seeing her cry. My chest tightens, and I want to hold her closer to me.

"I will only be gone for a few months. I will be back to raise our child together," I whisper. "It's only a matter of weeks—"

"Raja," Papa calls out from the living room.

"The food is getting cold. Both of you hurry up," Papa says annoyingly.

Haleema wipes the tears rolling down her face and checks her reflection in the window to see if the black kohl is smeared across her face. Fixing her hair from where I touched it, she pulls her scarf back over her head and walks into the dining room with her eyes drooping low.

Walking in behind her, I find my spot on the ground beside Papa, purposefully avoiding everyone's eyes. The enticing aroma of rice and lentils fills the air as I fixate on the pots in front of me. I eat silently, focusing on the grains clinging to my fingers. The spices sting my hand from where the birds peck at me. The stinging spreads to my tongue, paralyzing me with the anxiety of bringing up the news—that I will leave them, abandon them, and no longer sit with them during meals.

"Papa, Mama." The spices sting my throat as I conjure up the strength to speak.

Mama stares at me keenly. Lines surround her eyes and her white hairs poke out from under her scarf. Her eyes look at me as if to ask, "What is it, child?"

"Go on, my child," Papa says.

"Papa, I…" The heat spreads down to my stomach. "Salim bhai and the animals…" I stumble on my words. "Papa. I am going." I feel my heart beating in my throat. I am afraid they will hear my heart instead of my words.

"Go on, child. Where are we going?" Papa says, looking at me.

"I am going to America," I shout to ease the stinging, slow down the pain, and hush my brain.

Mama, Papa, and Haleema fall into an uneasy silence. Food drops from their hands with a heavy thud. The bustling sounds of vegetable vendors shouting out various prices seep into the room. The ceiling fan's ticking sound grows louder.

"Salim bhai is sending me to America with animals," I blurt out with my grip tightening around the glass of water. I gulp it down, desperately waiting for someone to break the silence.

Everyone remains quiet.

"America," Papa says. "How long will you be there?"

"Maybe a few weeks or months. I am unsure right now," I respond, wiping the sweat collecting above the groove of my lip.

"On a flight or—"

"I am going on a ship," I cut him off.

"A ship!" he cries. "Oh, child, you know these ships don't run that well. Your mother's brother sailed on one of those ships, and it never returned. They never found the ship. It sank." He shakes his head in disbelief.

"That was many years ago. These ships are better now. Besides, this is how Salim bhai sends his animals worldwide," I explain.

Silence fills the room again, making it impossible for me to discern Papa's true feelings.

"I trust that you have thought this through. You will be a big man now," Papa says while rubbing my back.

I observe his face to see if he really means it. He seems happy, mostly, though I see hints of concern.

"When do you leave, Raja?" Papa asks with tenderness in his voice.

"Friday, after prayer," Haleema and I glance at each other. Tears form in her eyes.

"Haleema, don't cry. I—"

"I'm not crying," she interrupts me. "It's these spice peppers, that's all." She avoids my gaze.

"We will all send you off proud." Papa's voice breaks.

"Salim bhai has trusted you with a task. He has seen you work hard all these years and is sending you to America. He knows you are an honest boy, incapable of making mistakes." Papa's eyes water.

"You have made your father very proud," he says, still rubbing my back.

He rises slowly from his spot, hiding his tears in our presence. He distances himself from his half-eaten meal, unable to articulate his emotions. Haleema collects Papa's plate and her plate and retreats to the kitchen.

Mama is silent. Not a single word escapes her lips. I listen closely, praying for even a sigh, anything that'll tell me what she's thinking. We are left behind with our plates in front of us.

And then, as though heeding my looks, she asks, "Have you thought through this decision?" Her tone is firm and her scrutinizing gaze narrows upon me, almost as though she is interrogating me.

"Yes, Mama." I nod. "I will leave Friday," I say, lowering my eyes, unable to meet her piercing glare.

She remains wordless, rising abruptly and abandoning the pots and pans left in front of us. As she shuffles away, I hear her mumbling prayers under her breath. "Ya Allah, protect my son."

Her words echo in my ears as I contemplate my decision. Have I thought through this decision? I have to take advantage of this opportunity. Don't I? I know my mother needs me near her, but I can't turn this down just to sit in her lap all day.

I must take this chance, even if it means leaving them behind. I must do this. It's the only way.

CHAPTER 3

CARROM

———

March 13, 1988

The screeching sounds of peacocks echo through the streets, mingling with the clicking of the ceiling fan and jolting me awake every morning. The fan's spinning panels tremble, rattling beneath a brown spot caused by rainwater seeping through the roof. It feels as if the whole house has been shaking like the fan since I broke the news of my departure.

As I nestle in bed, the mattress cradles me in its soft sheets. With my feet hanging off the edge, I cling to Haleema, holding on to her as if for dear life. I bury my face in her rose-scented hair. I want to shatter the shackles of time, free us from its restraints, and cherish her precious body in my arms forever.

Just a few more moments, I beg silently with the hands of the clock.

Haleema remains sound asleep as light illuminates through the cracks of the opaque window. The warm rays of the sun dance along her tempting body. I sweep her deep black hair out of her face with my fingers and plant a kiss on her forehead benignly, not wanting to wake her up. The aroma of dried leaves with hints of cloves from her henna-dyed hair fills my nostrils as I move closer to her. Her beauty is effortless. As I push her shirt off, revealing her smooth velvet skin, I kiss her swollen stomach, succumbing to her irresistible allure.

I feel her slender fingers run through my hair as I kiss her stomach, lowering myself graciously on her while making sure not to put my weight on her to protect her stomach and our child. My heart races, craving more of her. I cover her tawny body with my wet kisses as I move down her stomach.

Gently, I place my ear on her belly, trying to hear our baby. I can only hear the sounds of her stomach swishing. I lie unperturbed, thinking about the life I want to give this child. The money I will get by delivering these animals will grant a better life for our child. There will be no more brown stains, cracked windows, or old ceiling fans shaking.

Gold bangles wrap around her delicate wrists, ringing as they hit against each other. They are the same bangles her mother wore and have now been passed down to her elegant arms. I was unable to gift her with gold for our wedding. We could barely feed all the wedding guests my father invited to my wedding.

I play with her gold bracelets and hear them ring as they hit against each other. I want her to have more. She deserves more than I can provide for her.

Haleema pushes my head off her stomach and moves away from me. She shuts her puffy eyelids tightly.

It's time to rise, but today is different. I don't have to rush to the farm this morning. It's my one day off.

I'm unsure where the road will lead.

Haleema props herself up on her elbow. Tears collect in her eyes, inducing me to rest her head on my shoulder. I have no words. The pain I am causing her makes me feel like I'm ripping my own heart apart. She resists for a second and then gives in.

She lifts her head from my shoulder, and tenderly, I cradle her face in my hands, bestowing a gentle kiss on her rosy nose. Tears cascade down her cheeks. A surge of anguish grips my heart as I see her distress.

"Everything will be fine, Haleema," I whisper, my voice hoarse. I cuddle her ruddy face to my chest.

She remains silent, gracefully rising from the bed and making her way to the loose handle of the wardrobe. As she pulls it open, the door emits a high-pitched squeak. Her hand reaches for her scarf, a constant companion, as she swiftly exits the room. The lingering presence of the fan still shakes.

She walks away, further and further from me, into the rest of the house, undisturbed, as though nothing bothers her. Like clockwork, she is off to her daily chores, solely responsible for preparing breakfast for everyone.

Meanwhile, the heavy weight of dread lies beside me in the bed, marked by damp spots left on my shirt by her tears. The urge to sob tugs at my heart, but I shield my emotions and find the strength to abandon my bed.

I make my way into the dining area and stir my cup of tea in a circle to avoid the cream collecting on the surface.

I watch the swiftness of Haleema moving around the house, dusting the shelves and surfaces. My father shakes the water can while tending to his plants. My brothers Siraj and Rizwan argue over what to listen to on the radio. My sister flips through the newspaper, playing with her long braid in her lap. I grasp every last second left here, wringing the memories out of the day.

"Raja," Papa interrupts my observations.

"Don't you need to get going?" He reminds me of the several tasks ahead—my household duties and preparing for an unknown journey.

"Yes, I am just about to head out," I reassure him.

I embark on a trip to Empress Market to buy a suitcase and a few Western clothes. Amid the concrete walls, the market once served as a place for the British to sell spices and goods to each other. Now it is a clothing market filled with blue jeans, sneakers, and T-shirts with foreign city names printed on them. Empress Market has boxes of secondhand clothes.

British names still linger on plaques above the entrance of the market. The bell tower stands strong, forever ringing through these streets. Despite its chimes that toll faithfully every hour, its rings often succumb to the blaring of car horns and vendors yelling out prices.

Amid the noise, I hear the bell tower as it strikes three times. Time is racing. If only I could pause it and hold on to these last few moments I have left in my city.

I approach a stall, and my gaze sweeps over the array of clothes on display. They appear constricting, like they'd be suffocating against my skin. The denim feels coarse and lacks silkiness and elegance like my traditional clothes. I try on different pairs of pants, oblivious to what size would fit me. I've only had my clothes tailored to my measurements.

I buy denim jeans, button-downs, sneakers, a leather belt, and a sturdy suitcase to keep all my belongings. Owing to our circumstances, no one in my family has ever left the city to live elsewhere. Even when Haleema moved to my home last year, she carried her belongings in red and white striped plastic bags.

The impending journey looms before me. I am ill-prepared. I possess meager funds. And now, my child will arrive soon. I can't squander money on unwanted clothes.

Gathering my belongings, I depart from the bustling market streets and enter the narrow alleyways before emerging into another busy road to catch the bus home. Several buses pass before me, leaving a cloud of black and gray smoke behind them, each filled with people. Gasoline lingers in the air, and people shove each other to get on the bus. While waiting, my head throbs. I grip my suitcase tightly, afraid the bustle will sweep away everything, including my belongings.

I push away from the crowd and stand beside an older man by the bus stop. He looks at me with an expression of some familiarity, as if he recognizes me from somewhere. He is of meager size and dressed in the same Western clothes I just bought—a white button-down shirt with the first few buttons undone, revealing his white chest hair. I turn to greet him.

"Asalam Alaykum," I say with a slight bow. He smiles at the suitcase and twists his wrist, questioning what the bag is for.

"I am going abroad," I tell him, torn between whether I should answer truthfully or not. Perhaps he won't believe me.

"America?" he asks.

"Yes," I reply, my brows furrowing. How did he guess? Many young men like me are itching to go abroad.

"My son recently left, too," he shares, averting his gaze. His Urdu carries a particular accent that I can't distinguish. Ethnically he looks Sindhi, like most of the people here in Karachi. But his Urdu lacks the typical traces of Sindhi.

"I… uh… I lived in America for a long, long time. It was a wonderful country," the old man stutters.

"It's… uh… it's a different world," he says now in English, clear and crisp as the Americans might speak.

"Do you still live there?" I ask inquisitively.

The old man chuckles a bit before saying, "Ah yes, once you enter that country, there's no point returning."

Before I can say anything further, a shiny black car arrives, and he vanishes like a bird flying away into the sky.

What type of world can it be?

While waiting for the bus, Ali bhai, a rickshaw driver from our neighborhood in Nazimabad, pulls over in front of me. If the older man were still here, I would have offered to take him home, allowing me to ask him more questions.

"Get in, Raja. I am heading home," Ali bhai insists.

"No, it's okay. The bus will be here." I politely decline but hope he continues to insist.

"I'm heading to see your father anyway. Don't argue with me," Ali bhai says as he steps out and grabs my things.

We load my belongings into the rickshaw and are soon on the way. The engine roars to life, drowning out my thoughts while plumes of black clouds gather ominously behind us.

"Your father mentioned your departure, Raja." He raises his voice against the cacophony of honking horns in the bustling streets.

"Yes, I am leaving soon," I reply. A wave of remorse washes over me.

"We are proud of you, Raja. I have seen you as a child taking care of your family. Good deeds do not go unnoticed. Allah is rewarding you and sending you abroad. You will be a big man one day," Ali bhai says.

"God willing," I say in return, hoping his kind wo
to fruition.

As we continue our journey back home, a heavy
overcomes me. Ali bhai focuses on the road ahead, ar
old man's words haunt me, his presence leaving me with
lingering questions. Why did he return to Karachi? I mull
over what the old man said about there being no point
in returning.

We reach my home just in time for prayer, and the bustling street comes alive with the sounds of local vendors setting up their carts. It's a familiar scene. After prayers, men
gather on the roads, eager to indulge in the savory snacks
offered by the vendors.

Leaving my suitcase inside the gate of our house, I hurry
over to the mosque upon hearing the azan. As I perform
wuzu, I scan the crowd, hoping to catch a glimpse of Papa.
He must already be in the first row, so I find my place among
the prayer rugs.

The imam recites a few verses from the Quran and shares
a story with us. He tells us about how, as the Prophet would
enter the mosque, there would always be a man who taunted
him every day and made derogatory comments about him
and his prayer. One day, the Prophet noticed the absence
of this man. To his surprise, he found the man unwell. The
Prophet, with a generous heart, brought the man food and
medicine. The imam emphasized the importance of following the Prophet's example and extending such generosity
to others.

We have a duty to take care of one another. It is part of
what makes us Muslim, and it is part of what makes our
community and faith stronger. We are all here to provide

and support one another. I hope to find people as generous—people I can rely on for help.

"Bismillah Al-Rehman Nir Raheem," in the name of God, the most gracious, the most merciful, the imam resounds. His mellifluous voice flows through the loudspeakers, embracing the hearts of us worshipers.

Our heads bow to the floor at his call. I keenly feel the weight of my family resting upon my shoulders, anchoring me to the soft Persian rug beneath my forehead. As the imam's voice carries through the air, I feel tranquil, causing my eyes to water.

As prayer comes to an end, I remain on the floor, holding my face in my hands and seeking a moment to myself. I ask Allah to protect my family while I am away. I ask for nothing more but their safety.

Suddenly, I feel the gentle warmth of a hand resting on my shoulder. I turn to find Papa standing above me.

"Did you get everything?" he asks, brushing some dirt off my face with the back of his fingers.

"Yes, Papa," I respond, unable to meet his gaze.

"Go home and rest. You look tired," Papa pats my head and points toward the door.

I head home as Papa stops to buy fresh samosas and salty fried dough shaped like trapezoids. When he enters the house, the smell of the fried salty snacks fills the room.

Haleema rushes to grab the plastic bags with snacks wrapped in newspaper and places them on white and blue plates. She prepares tea and mixes cardamom, cloves, and cinnamon into the loose-leaf tea, filling the kitchen with the aroma of warm spices. She pokes a hole in the milk bag and drains it into the pot, where the water boils. I bring out a few cups with the samosas, walk into the living room, and find my hungry brothers and sister waiting for the snacks.

My brother, Siraj, sets up the carrom board, ready for another game against me. Taking the black and white tiles from the box, Siraj aligns them in a circle in the center of the carrom board.

I sit on the opposite side of Siraj for a game of carrom— one of the only games we play for hours without breaking our concentration.

Carrom is played best with two players. Siraj sprinkles some powder and tiny bits of pink sand on the board to allow the strikers to glide better. He places the red queen in the middle and surrounds her with black and white tiles.

Flicking the striker with my fingers, I hit the tiles in the middle, breaking the formation. One black tile makes its way into one of the four corner holes. I look around the board to see which one I can slide into the corner next. Nothing is perfectly lined up for me. The striker glides across the board, hitting the edge and missing the tiles.

It's Siraj's turn now. I see the focus in his eyes as his head leans closer to the board to eye where the striker will hit. He flicks the piece and gets a white tile in the hole. He is much more focused and precise with his shots than I am. I can't keep up with him and his accuracy.

We take turns striking the board and pausing to sip our tea. At the end of our game, Siraj places the tiles back in the middle instead of cleaning them up.

"When are you leaving, bhaijaan?" he asks, referring to me as his older brother formally and respectfully.

"I will be gone later this week," I say with the striker in my palm.

"When you leave, I will be the oldest in the house." He chokes a bit on his words, pauses, and turns his gaze away, looking down at his hands. "But I will never be able to take care of everyone the way you have all these years." He chokes again and looks at the floor.

I lower my head and avoid looking at his teary eyes. My mouth feels dry again, and I am at a loss for words of comfort. I place the striker on the board. It glides on its own, slowly due to the powder and sand on the board.

"You are more capable than you think," I reassure him.

"You are focused on the board and understand the different angles," I remind him. "I know you will understand the needs of our family. You will know when to approach others and understand what everyone needs. Part of this game is also trying to anticipate the other player's moves. Taking care of people is the same way, Siraj. Anticipate Papa and Mama's needs, and you will always win." I walk away before my own eyes shed tears.

The thought of leaving everyone unprepared fills me with worry. I attend to their every need, and now they will have to learn to fend for themselves.

Regret slowly seeps into my heart as I walk to my room. But it is the right choice.

CHAPTER 4

DEPARTURE

———

March 18, 1988

Tigers are always the hardest to feed. Raw chunks of meat are sliced and dumped into buckets every few days.

I plop the wet slimy pieces of meat between the metal rods, sure never to unlock the door. They smell the meat before I squeeze it through the metal bars and scratch the cages, unwilling to wait patiently for their meal.

"Wait a minute! Be patient," I call out to the animals while placing their food.

We have many tigers to feed, but we house them in separate cages since they aren't always fond of sharing their meals and end up attacking and scratching one another.

I have worked with animals since childhood without ever being attacked or bitten by any of them. They have grown familiar to my scent, recognizing me as one of their own. I try to decipher their unspoken messages. Within the confines of the Al-Ahmed Animal House, life unfolds in its cyclical pattern as some depart and new animals arrive—a perpetual cycle.

In the quiet hours of early morning, before the sun's ascent, I arrive earlier than usual to identify which animals will bid farewell today. Later this evening, they will board a ship and sail away for hundreds of miles to a new home that bears no resemblance to the home they leave behind. An unsettling sensation lingers in my mind regarding how they will be cared for.

In this sanctuary, we indulge our animals, ensuring their well-being and treating them with the utmost care and compassion. Under my watchful eye, no animal has died of disease or starvation. I tend to these animals as I would my own kin. Yet I find myself pondering over their fate in the hands of others. Will they be treated well? Will they remain unharmed?

Even Muslims' meat is adequately taken care of. Proper food and diet are given to animals to make them healthy for us to eat. We ensure the cows, goats, and lambs are unharmed and given fresh food. When it's time for their slaughter, we adhere to the tenets of halal, ensuring a swift and humane process by cutting their necks and allowing the blood to flow. Torturing these animals, who provide sustenance, would contradict the halal principles.

I linger for a while, eagerly anticipating the arrival of Salim bhai. My patience pays off as I see Salim bhai gradually approaching with someone else, an unfamiliar man. The foreign man stands out. His Western attire diverges from the traditional clothes worn here. He's wearing a white button-down cotton shirt paired with navy blue silky pants. His hair gracefully dances in the wind as he walks, and his mustache gently dangles from his face.

The man carries a clipboard, clutching it firmly in his hands. Attached to it are several papers flying with the wind.

Salim bhai walks over, and I shake the hand of the unfamiliar man too.

"This is Abrar," Salim bhai says.

"He is going to help us load the animals on the ship," Salim bhai says as his eyes gleam with pride. One of his most profitable endeavors must be a shipment to the West.

"Abrar has helped ship all of our animals. I know you usually don't deal with this, Jahangir, but we will need your help this time." Salim bhai puts his hands on my shoulder. It feels warm and sweaty.

We walk to the cage, where I mark the animals that will go on the ship. Bright orange plastic paper strips are looped through the cells and tied to mark them for shipment.

I leave the two men, but just as I do so, I hear them talking about the animals and the business. Abrar asks how much each tiger is worth, but I can't hear Salim bhai's answer as I walk away far enough.

These animals don't mean the same to Salim bhai as they do to me; it's not about making a profit.

I wait by the bird cages, still thinking about how much the tigers must bring for Salim bhai. It smells of animal waste. Tiny feathers are scattered throughout the area as the birds flap their wings. A part of me wants to release the hundreds of colorful parakeets. I want to tell them to fly away and never come back. The birds sing loudly in their cages. I, too, want to fly free, for a time, away from responsibilities.

Rectangular white cages of the same size are stacked on top of each other like a brick wall of bird homes. There are about five parakeets per cage and hundreds of cells. Aziz is already by the bird section. He deftly pulls out the trays under the cages to wash away the stains and the black and white waste.

"Jahangir bhai, you are going to America today. How do you feel?" he asks with a smile across his face.

"I'm a bit nervous," I respond, not looking at him but staring at the parakeets flying around in the cages, still tempted to set them free. Aziz never needed to decide to leave or not. I was the only one who ultimately had to make the decision. "Aziz, didn't you want to go?" I ask.

"Oy, Jahangir bhai, I told Salim bhai I couldn't go. I have everything I want here and several weeks on the ship, and you know my English isn't good. I failed English in my metric exams," he says while hosing down the trays. Water splashes on his shirt.

"I just didn't want to miss my first child being born. Who knows how many days those Americans would make me work there, and I don't even know anyone," he says while fidgeting with his collar in one hand.

"I'm not sure if I should go," I blurt out, revealing more to Aziz than I want to.

"It will be a few months, and then you will be here with me. Feeding these birds and taking care of the animals again." Aziz taps the tray and leans them against the cement wall to dry.

"I didn't want to go searching for something bigger or better. Sometimes in search of something better, we lose what we have closest to us. I am happy here, truthfully," Aziz says as he pinches his neck at the word truthfully, implying the honesty in his words.

"Anyway, at the end of the day, jahan chah wahan raah— *hard work pays off*," Aziz says as he wraps the remaining orange plastic tags around the cage doors.

"God willing, your hard work will pay off," I say. Aziz is happy here. If given the choice, he would turn down the opportunity to leave. Am I making the wrong decision by taking these animals? Should I not go?

I hush my thoughts. Now is not the time to be doubtful. I will not be gone for long.

"You know what to do. I'm going to head home. I need to reach the port tonight," I say, touching Aziz's shoulder. His slender frame is fragile. I fear that even a strong breeze could knock him off balance, his bones delicate and his body gaunt.

Although my work remains unfinished, I must return home and gather my belongings to ensure I arrive at the port on time. Numerous family members will gather, offering prayers for my safe journey.

I walk home with my hands in my pockets, playing with my keys. As I step through the front door, an unsettling sensation courses through me. Fatigue and pain from the day weigh heavily upon me. My mind feels hazy, in a fog, struggling to comprehend the reality of leaving everything behind. Thoughts of my departure haunt my every step.

I slide my hand down, feeling the cold metallic handle, and gently pull it. I hear that old familiar latch click open again. I walk inside this empty home. The tiles are cold, and the ash of chamomile incense collects in a reddish clay pot near the door. The fan is shaking, causing a loud echoing sound. Everyone must be at the market, gathering food for the evening meal.

Wings flapping and pigeons landing along the balcony welcome me home. I take a few steps on the cold white porcelain tiles and grab the bird feed. The pigeons are always on time for their meal. Their gray feathers float throughout the house. Their bodies rest on the shelves I built. I toss a handful of seeds from the bucket on the shelves for the pigeons to eat. This will be the last day I feed them. Will I ever return to this again?

Hopefully, someone remembers to feed them while I am gone. Otherwise, they will fly away and find another home and place to feed from—far away from here.

How does time move so quickly? A bell strikes my head every hour, reminding me that time is ticking. No sooner than Salim bhai mentioned America, the day of my departure crept upon me.

I carefully pack my final belongings into my bag. As I arrange the items, my eyes settle on Papa's Quran and janamaz, which I place on top. The janamaz has imprints of my father's footsteps etched into its fabric from years of intense prayer. The callus on his forehead is evidence of his discipline in praying multiple times daily. With these tangible reminders, the rug becomes a precious memento, inspiring me to follow in his footsteps and maintain my prayer routine.

Trying to focus on the task, I realize I need my shoes. "Haleema," I call out, knowing she typically puts my shoes away. Usually, they are beneath the bed.

"Yes?" she says while running toward our room from the kitchen, abandoning the tea on the stove.

Her face looks completely different. Her eyes are droopy, and her nose is red around the edges from crying. Her eyes are puffy with no more tears left to give. I look away, unable to complete a thought or remember where things are. I cannot bear to see her this way.

"I can't find my shoes, Haleema. Where did you put them?" I ask sternly, annoyed by her.

"Janab, they are right under the bed," she says as she walks to the other end of the bed. She begins to bend over, but I stop her, not wanting her to crush our child while leaning toward the ground.

Reaching for the black shoes under the dusty bed, I find other old items and a box with our albums from our wedding. A wave of hesitancy rushes through my body, leaving goosebumps behind. I freeze in my spot. Our wedding was a celebration of love. Now I am leaving the one I love behind.

"What's wrong, my love?" Haleema asks.

I quickly come back to my senses, the goosebumps leaving my body. Now is not the time to look at them and regret my decision to leave.

"Nothing. I can't seem to reach the box." My voice muffles as I crawl under the bed.

Dust covers the box. I haven't worn these nice shoes since my wedding. I grab the shoes from the box and polish them with black polish and an old rag. Haleema sits next to me. She avoids my eyes, taking the right shoe from the box instead. Rubbing the black liquid over the shoe, she makes them shine. These should last me a few days on the ship until they fade away, adjusting to the environment.

I slide my feet into the shiny black shoes, usually worn on special celebratory occasions. It's time to say goodbye to Haleema. My head drops down to my chest, and I hold it in my hands. Haleema places her skinny hands around my face and pulls my head closer to her chest. Her heart is beating fast. I feel her fingers running through my hair. Tears form in my eyes. I turn my gaze away quickly. I can't cry in front of Haleema. I am the man. She should not be the one consoling me. Lifting my head, I place her head on my shoulders.

"You are the reason my heart beats," she repeats one of the lines of poetry. "And only for you will it beat."

I can say nothing to her. Seeing her this way, knowing it is my doing, makes my chest tight. We slowly unwind from each other. My hands run through her long black silky hair. She wraps her hair on her head several times and covers her head with her red scarf.

She uses the ends of her scarf to wipe away her tears, revealing her stomach and our child.

"Beta, are you all packed and ready?" Papa peers into the doorway. Haleema quickly moves away from me, readjusting her shirt.

"Yes, Papa. I am ready," I say, looking toward the ground. I avoid making eye contact, afraid I will burst into tears.

As I walk through the house, I notice the home is quieter than usual, lacking the lively energy when our family gathers. Relatives quietly shuffle into the house; their footsteps echo as the door opens and greetings are exchanged. An array of shoes fills the entryway. The clinking of teacups hitting their plates reverberates through the hallway, adding to the atmosphere. People have gathered to bid me farewell and offer their wishes for the journey ahead.

I embrace everyone individually, and they whisper the words of Allah in my ear. Tears flow freely down my aunts' faces. When I reach Mama, I find her head covered with her shawl as she wipes away tears with trembling fingers.

"Don't forget to recite the prayer for travel," she says as she caresses my face with her soft hands. Her fingers are fragile, and her bangles slide down her arms as she reaches for the top of my head. Mama kisses my forehead, leaving dampness behind. I rest her head on my shoulder and kiss the back of her head. I hear her weep a bit more. She never thought I would one day leave, even if my return is anticipated. But to my family, they doubt I will ever return from the foreign land.

Papa separates us and gestures for me to walk to the door. I can still feel her hands gripping my shirt as we slowly move away from each other. My cousins take my bags and head to the car.

Once inside the car, I settle in the backseat with Haleema, Papa, and Siraj as we embark on our journey to the port. The streets of Karachi appear exceptionally enchanting today, adorned with Urdu graffiti on cement bridges and walls and bearing heartfelt lines about love and the importance of family. When we come to a red light, a few beggars approach the car asking for money in exchange for prayers and well wishes. I hand over a few coins, hoping their prayers will come in handy. If not for me, for the tiny piece of life growing in Haleema's stomach.

When the smell of the ocean hits our senses, Haleema and I look at each other with small, gentle smiles. We know these are our final minutes together until I depart on the ship. The strong gust of winds restricts our path as we approach the cargo ship. The ship looks like a massive building floating on water. How something so big and powerful can float on water doesn't make sense. The smell of smoke fills the area. People yell directions at each other as the last few containers load to sail across the world.

As we arrive on the dock, Salim bhai is already there. He waves at me, signaling me to walk over to him.

"Salam, Salim bhai," I say, shaking his hand.

"Jahangir, the ship has already docked the animals. You will be able to get access to the animals and need to feed them on the cycle. This badge will help you get around the ship easier, and no one will ask many questions." Salim bhai hands me a necklace with a small rectangular card that has my name and the ship's name on it.

I collect my belongings from my cousins and hug Haleema, afraid to show her too much affection in front of my family. I want to hold on to her forever. If only I could take her with me.

Turning to my father, he wraps his hands around my back. I can't remember the last time we embraced this way.

"Raja, you have made me so proud," he whispers in my ear as he softly weeps to himself, holding my face with both hands.

"I brought you home with these two hands. Now these two hands are sending you off to be a bigger man," he says, looking into my eyes. Tears collect on my face, and he wipes them off with his strong but gentle thumbs.

"Go, child. We will miss you," he says. His nimble fingers grab a gray and black plaid handkerchief from his pocket to blow his nose. The golden glow on his face fades as sorrow fills his eyes.

Standing on the ship, I look over the edge and wave goodbye, but my family is out of sight. I relentlessly wave until the horizon is only a line, and the sound of waves crashing against the ship floods my ears. The smell of Papa's cologne still lingers on my shirt.

CHAPTER 5

WHITE TIGER

—

March 19, 1988

The ship makes me shiver as if an ice cube is gliding down my back. Its frigid walls go on forever, like a mansion of silver walls. An endless amount of steel surrounds me at any given moment. It's hard to imagine going from life with the animals, out in the blazing sun, smelling the cow waste around me, to now smelling the salty ocean surrounding me. This cargo ship is one of the largest ships with containers to supply food to other countries. I wonder what this ship has brought on board from Pakistan besides the animals. Raw cotton, jeans, and several dozen textiles truckers were lined up on the coast to board the ship. Who else might be aboard?

"Oy, sisterfucker get back downstairs. Your shift isn't over," someone yells and cusses in Urdu. I walk over to where I hear the voice. I see a small, short man with a thick beard and the ends of his mustache curled. His long curly hair rests on his shoulders.

I walk into the room and see a group of men sitting in a circle drinking out of white foam cups. "Are you Pakistani?" the hairy man asks, squinting his eyes.

"Jahangir," I say my name as I extend out my hand.

"Saife," he responds and shakes my hands. Blisters and rough patches cover his hands.

"Where are you from in Pakistan?" I ask, but I know he's from Punjab because of his accent.

"I'm from Lahore. I can see the Badshahi mosque from my rooftop," Saife says. "And you... are you from Karachi?"

"Yes, I joined the ship today with a few animals," I immediately regret my answer. Why would a man like me be traveling with animals?

Saife's inky eyebrows furrow.

I stumble over my words. "Zoo animals. I'm bringing them to America. I work at this place that takes care of animals before shipping them worldwide."

"There are a few animals on this ship too. Including me. What types of animals do you have?" Saife asks. His wavy hair glistens as he pushes it out of his face.

"Mainly birds like parakeets and parrots. But this customer wanted more than birds. I have a white tiger. You can hear them when you walk by the cages," I ramble. I pause to remember the sounds of the birds chirping and singing in the morning at the zoo.

"Stop it. There's no way a tiger is on this ship, and you are about to drop it off to some rich snob American. How is it going to eat?" Saife says in utter disbelief. Again, he pushes his long hair out of his face, grabbing a handful and pushing it back or running his rugged fingers through it.

"I can show you. Do you want to join me tomorrow morning when I feed the animals? Where are you staying?"

"I don't stay where the rest of you stay. I'm in the engine room and stay with the engineers," Saife says.

"I'll come down to the engine room tomorrow morning and bring you to where the animals are," I say as I shake his tough blister-covered hands again. The labor of this ship is wearing on his fingers.

I leave Saife engrossed in his work and ascend through the various levels of the ship, making my way back to my quarters. Along the journey, I traverse a labyrinth of countless containers within the cargo hold, catching glimpses of the designated areas for the ship's crew, captain, and even the captain's family. The air is laced with the scent of metal, mingling with a faint hint of oil and the distant hum of machinery. Every segment of the ship is distinctively segregated, restricted by the occupants' roles and intentions. In the quarters allocated for the dedicated workers, I catch the rhythmic clatter of tools, accompanied by snippets of laughter. As I venture further, I approach the private domain of the captain and his family. Here, the air carries the delicate fragrance of polished wood.

As the ship heaves with the relentless waves, I stumble to my cramped quarters. Fumbling with the key, I force the door open. The steel walls seem to close in on me, trapping me like a caged animal. The ceiling is low, and I must duck my head to walk around. There are no windows to let in the fresh sea breeze. I breathe the stale air in my claustrophobic room.

I collapse onto the narrow mattress. My mind fills with memories of Haleema. I can hear her voice, feel her soft hair against my face, and sense her warm body as if we were lying together. I imagine her back against my chest, the soothing sounds of her breathing. I picture our unborn child wriggling around in her stomach as my hand rests on her belly button.

For a moment, I'm in a place of warmth and safety. But then the parrot in my room violently flaps her wings, lurching me off my bed. My dream shatters, and I am left alone, stuck in my metal cage.

The following day, I make my way to the cafeteria for breakfast. Cornflakes, rice, beans, and an array of unfamiliar boxed items greet me. The distinct aroma of eggs lingers in the air. There is no trace of *paratha* or *halwa* today. I reluctantly pick up a plate of bright yellow, mushed-up eggs and some bread.

The eggs are dripping, and the bread is stiff. The texture feels oddly uniform, lacking richness and creaminess, as I reluctantly bite. I force myself to consume the tasteless food before me, mindlessly mashing the eggs and barely taking a few bites before gulping them down. Like a caged animal, I attack my meal, my impatient stomach denying my mouth the pleasure of savoring each morsel.

As the time to feed the animals approaches, I make my way through the ship's depths, venturing down into the heart of the engine room to find Saife. The pungent odor of oil and gas assaults my senses. How can Saife work in these conditions? There aren't any lights down here, leaving me reliant solely on the feeble glow emanating from the machines. There aren't any windows, only massive equipment making the ship move.

After asking a few people for Saife, I hear his distinct voice in the distance.

"I can work the night shift every day until we get to America, and then I'll work during the day. One of the nights, I will make my escape. I won't get back on the ship. When they look for me, say you heard me go to the bathroom," I overhear Saife saying in Urdu to another engineer.

He sees me and stops talking. "Hey, zookeeper! You ready to show me a tiger?" he asks and wipes the thick sweat off of his face.

It's dark and musty in the engine room. The sounds of pipes and alarms go off amid a constant ticking sound of metal hitting metal. It's hard for me to make out the words Saife is saying.

"Do you want to see some animals?" I shout.

We walk up the stairs toward where the animals are stored. I unlock the container with the food and measure out the portions. Counting one, two, three, I ensure the buckets are filled. I pile the buckets onto a cart and wheel them to the animals' cages. Saife is quiet throughout the process as his eyes dart around the area. Perhaps he is overwhelmed by the realization that the ship he works for carries food distributed throughout the world and houses animals.

"Open that hinge right there." I point to the container with the animals. "And turn it to your left, and when you hear the clicking sound pull the door open."

Saife figures it out relatively easily. After all, he is an engineer. It's easy for him to understand the mechanics of doors and levers. Hopefully, it's easy for him to understand the mechanics of animals.

As he unlocks the door, inside is a large cage behind the pillars and door rests a white tiger. His eyes twitch from the light as he slowly walks toward us, recognizing me. His eyes ask me why I have put him in this cage. Where are the others? I try to look away from his eyes, knowing I have put him in this cage, in the dark, away from his home.

"Wow!" Saife's eyes light up. "You weren't lying. There really is a tiger on this ship," Saife says as he approaches the cage. He touches the poles on the cage.

"I wouldn't get too close. The tiger isn't happy with me today and might want to take out his revenge," I say.

"How can you tell if he's happy or not?" Saife asks, still in astonishment.

"The animals do not have a voice. It is the job of us zookeepers to speak for the voiceless. I observe his actions," I tell Saife while walking to the massive container housing the tiger.

"I know when he is about to attack, his entire body will shift back with his front shoulders raised high. When hungry, he will pace the gate or bite the door. And right now, he didn't even acknowledge me. He feels betrayed, as if I have put him in a situation he doesn't want to be in," I say as I walk over to the front of the cage and start to unlock it.

"You're going to let him out?" Saife says with fear in his voice.

"Of course not. I don't want any accidents," I say.

I walk inside the cage and wait for him to notice me. He still has his head down, looking away as if I don't exist. His soft fur shines where the light hits.

"I'm sorry I am taking you somewhere else." I wait for him to listen. I am sure Saife must think I have lost my mind. I keep my focus on the tiger. Slowly, I take a few steps closer with one hand out. I am inching closer and closer until I feel his soft fur. My hand is about to touch him when the tiger suddenly pounces in the cage.

"Jahangir!" Saife screams from behind.

"It's okay! He is just taking his anger out on me. He won't hurt me," I say with two tiger paws on my shoulders. He growls, opening his enormous mouth to reveal his teeth as drool drips inside.

"I know you are mad. I am sorry." I bring my hands up, but the animal's weight is unmatched. I push free from his grasp by tossing my body on its side.

The tiger scratches the side of my stomach, piercing through my skin and flesh. I want to scream and yell, but I know that will terrify Saife. I hold the tiger's face and smack his nose. The tiger jerks his head and slowly returns to where he was lying. His claws scratch the bottom of the cage as he walks away.

I touch the side of my stomach to make sure I am not bleeding. Warm liquid covers my hand as blood trickles down my ribs, droplets collecting on the floor.

I hurry out of the cage with my head feeling like it's about to snap off from hanging low from the misery. Why have I locked these animals up? Saife is still there even after seeing me attacked by the tiger.

"Well, how'd you like the show?" I ask awkwardly, trying to mask my fear.

Saife stands there, speechless, his eyes and mouth wide open, completely frozen. I cautiously inch closer, but he backs away.

It's not so much the animal he fears but me. Before I can say anything, Saife scurries away. He runs toward the exit without looking behind him. He probably thinks of me as some lunatic with zoo animals on a ship.

I try to run after him, but the pain grows on my side as more blood rushes through my shirt. I fall to my knees, unable to bear the pain.

CHAPTER 6

CARGO

___

March 20, 1988

The next morning, I search for Saife at breakfast as a soggy mess of cornflakes sits before me, untouched, soaking up the milk. Similar to how I feel, soaking up my embarrassment. The side of my stomach still aches from the scratch. I rub the area slightly to calm the burning sensation piercing my ribs. I wonder if this massive ship has a doctor so I can get some proper bandages.

As I continue to linger, the hope of his arrival diminishes, and it dawns on me that he may not be intentionally avoiding me. He might be occupied in the engine room, diligently tending to his duties. I set off in search of him toward the engine room.

Navigating through the ship's corridors, I can't help but notice the uncanny similarity they all share. The steel walls are like a maze.

The smell—that pungent scent of oil and gas—overwhelms me again. There are so many sounds of shuffling and alarms going off. I don't know if this is the same area I had seen Saife before. The place seems to go on forever with no end in sight.

I hear the faint sounds of vulgar Urdu words. Saife must be nearby. His voice echoes in the engine room and several other noises.

"Saife," I yell, rushing into the room.

"Oy, Jahangir. How are you doing? I was telling these guys about what you showed me yesterday," he says. To my surprise, he seems genuinely happy to see me, even though I doubted it.

"I'm doing alright," I point to the side of my stomach.

"*Chalo*—let's go." He grabs my arm and walks me out of the room. "Come with me. I will make you some chai. I know you must be craving it," he says while walking me into a kitchen near the engine room. The words all slur together as he talks, not pausing for a second to catch his breath. The kitchen is noticeably smaller, lacking the grandeur and spaciousness of the cafeteria. It feels cozy and intimate with limited counter space and a compact layout.

Saife rattles the stove and pours some milk into an open-lid pot. He deftly adds loose tea, some cloves, cardamom, and cinnamon. Despite its modest size, the kitchen is well-equipped. Shelves and cabinets line the walls, filled with various pots, pans, and containers. Utensils hang from hooks above the stove.

"So, how are you adjusting to the ship, yar? It's lonely, I know. I wish I had a woman. Keep me company here and listen to me talk. I have to talk to these men here instead," Saife says rapidly. He speaks as if everything is a joke, taking nothing seriously.

"I miss my wife," I say, staring at the floor. "We are having a baby, and I feel as if I have left her at a bad time." I find myself sharing more information than I usually would with a stranger.

"Oh, I'm sure she'll be fine. Your family will look after her, no? I wouldn't worry too much," Saife says while stirring the bubbling liquid. The pot boils with steam collecting at the top. He hands me a warm mug of chai. The smell and the cup's warmth remind me of home.

"*Haan*—yes. She will be fine, but I'm worried. I have to take these animals, and by the time I return..."

"Return? You aren't planning to stay in the US?" Saife asks, cutting me off.

"No, I'm gonna go back. How could I stay? I don't have a visa either," I say.

"That's not a problem." Saife lets out a scuff.

"These days, there are many ways to get a visa or green card," Saife says, pausing to blow into his cup before taking a sip. He leans into me slowly and looks around the room to ensure no one is there.

"I'm gonna get off this ship and not get back on," he whispers.

"My cousin is there now, and I'll stay with him. He is on an education visa, and about ten other men live with him in his apartment; some have gotten visas through other ways. Some have married white women and paid them for the marriage license and the proof. Others have paid farmers to get them visas. There are so many ways to stay," Saife says while teasingly smacking my head.

I hadn't considered staying. I plan to deliver the animals and then return home, but I could stay longer. After I set up the animals in their new home, I could stay with the new owner and care for them.

"What will you do for work? You're making good money here on the ship," I ask him.

"Jobs are no issue. I'll work at the gas station or a store, and when my English improves, I will work at a better place. It doesn't happen overnight, but things work out," Saife says optimistically.

If there are easy ways to get a visa once I'm in the country, maybe I could stay.

* * *

Days turned into weeks, and weeks transformed into months as Saife and I share most of our meals. After taking care of the animals, I linger in the engine room, occasionally inviting the other Pakistani men working in the kitchen or engine room to join me in observing the animals on board.

When Saife finishes his shifts in the evenings, we gather with the other men to engage in games of spades, occasionally even placing bets with our hard-earned coins.

"How will we know when we arrive in Boston?" I ask Saife.

"Just like every other port we dock at," Saife replies, gesturing like a bird soaring through the air. "You hear it before you see it."

Confused, I press further, asking, "What do you mean?"

Saife chuckles and explains, "The seagulls. They're swarming and squawking. And since it's June, there will be even more seagulls flying."

"I guess I hadn't noticed the noises while docking. I was thrilled to be able to put my feet on land," I say.

"And with the port in Boston, you'll smell the salt mountains at the port," Saife says.

My stomach churns. I anticipated arriving and taking the animals to their new home and owners by land. I'm nervous to set foot in this foreign land and embark on the next part of the adventure. This will be the last time I see Saife since he will not return to the ship. This is his last stop too.

He perfectly planned it so that by the time we dock in Boston, his shift would end, and he would get to leave.

I gather my belongings, including the shiny black shoes I polished the day I left home, the parrot cage, and my suitcase. Saife told me to meet him by the ship's exit. I make my way to the door when I feel the ship dock.

I drag my things into the hallway. No longer will I need to feel these cold steel walls. The smell of the engine room will forever haunt me.

As I approach the exit, I ask the parrot, "Are you ready to see your new home?" But she remains completely silent.

We make our way to the exit, and I'm struck by the sheer number of people waiting in line to disembark. It's the most people I have seen. A lot have arrived by ship.

I notice people gathering their papers, passports, and cards to show at the exit. I do the same, checking my documents and finding the written instructions Salim bhai gave me. Saife doesn't have any of those things. I am not sure how he is going to get off.

Slap! I feel a hand on the back of my neck.

"I'm leaving!" Saife with a grin.

"Now remember, if you ever need anything, this is where I am staying." Saife hands me a piece of paper with an address and a few numbers followed by a street name I can't pronounce, the city, and a few more numbers:

19 Chauncy Street, #18 Cambridge, Massachusetts 02138.

I don't know how to even read this. I place the piece of paper in the pocket of my wallet; even if I never use the address, I will have it to keep as a memory of our friendship.

"Come visit me after you set up the zoo, and I'll make you some Lahori food. It will be so good you will lose your mind eating it," Saife says, fidgeting while bouncing up and down like a piece of popcorn in a machine. I caress his neck like one of my animals. A wave of sorrow fills my heart, causing my eyes to blink rapidly to keep my tears from falling.

"You have your ID and are ready to go?" I ask Saife as he is about to leave.

"I have my ID from Pakistan and some money in here." Saife pats his briefcase. "I'll show them the ID and say I'm just sending some money. And when they see that I am not taking any other stuff, just this ID and money, they will let me go and won't ask any questions. But I won't turn back. I will never get back on this ship," Saife says assuredly.

We embrace one last time, and a silent prayer for his protection escapes my lips. I watch him stride confidently to the exit. His determination is evident. Suddenly, a pale woman with golden hair stops him, and I observe him extracting some money from his pocket, explaining his urgent need to send it. They engage in a conversation, their words muffled by the atmospheric conditions. After a brief exchange, she grants him passage. The ship will remain docked at this port for several days, and it seems logical that people would disembark.

I watch him walk away in the distance, eventually blending in with the crowd.

Hours pass as the ship unloads its cargo at the bustling port of Boston. The loud beeping sound of trucks backing up and workers shouting commands fills my ear. The gentle breeze from the ocean feels distinct from the familiar sea view of home. As I breathe in the air, a unique blend of oil, petroleum, and the salty ocean mingles in my senses.

My attention is drawn to the countless cars passing by with their windows down and hands casually hanging out. The cars are noticeably larger than the ones back home, and they gleam with a polished shine, meticulously maintained. Judging by their size, they can accommodate far more people, unlike the back of my uncle's car, where we all squeezed in during my departure for the port.

As I sit by the dock and wait by the ship for my animals, I look at the massive land we are on. I could have never imagined what America looked like, which seemed very different from the movies I watched. Few white people are at the dock right now. I can't tell where the people are from, but they almost look like me—caramel-colored skin. Mocha eyes. Charcoal-colored hair. They are hard at work, unloading the cargo with massive cranes and machinery.

I wait for someone to approach me to confirm where my cargo is. I read over the tasks given by Salim bhai.

Wait for the cargo on the ship to completely unload before approaching one of the workers about where you need to go.

Based on the code, the port will know to send you on a truck with the container to its destination. The truck will not leave without you. I have already told them you will accompany the truck driver.

Contact me after you have reached the destination.

You will get back on the ship you came off of. The ship will stay at the port for about a week before returning to the Asia route.

I ask several people working, and they send me to other people to ask the same questions. I provide them with the name of the company I am representing and the content of the containers. I check to see if the containers are in the same spot as where I was feeding them, but they are nowhere to be found.

Finally, a man from the dock comes up to me. He is pale with a stern look on his face.

"Jahangir Rehman," he addresses me by my full name, enunciating each syllable with a thick American accent, making my name sound foreign to my ears.

"Yes?" I answer, a bit puzzled.

"I regret to inform you, but your cargo is missing."

"Missing?" I scream. How can it be missing? My stomach feels like it's in several knots. My head spins. The noises rush into my ears.

"But where are my animals? I've been waiting here all day." I feel my heart racing. "All the containers have just vanished?" I say as I feel my heart thumping in my chest harder and harder. I am shouting and out of breath. I feel like a fish out of water, unable to breathe.

"Sir, I have already told you," the white man says flatly. "The containers probably got mislabeled and mixed up. We can track your container, but the numbers you have written here are not in our log. We will try our best to look for them, and you can stay on the ship, but the ship will leave in a matter of days. I recommend you stay near the port somewhere."

I know no one here. No one for miles past the roads, past the ocean, past the buildings. If only Saife were here to help me. Saife. Saife is here!

"I know a man from the ship. I mean from here in Boston studying at the college to become a doctor," I quickly try to correct myself not to give away too much information. Boston must have many colleges and students studying to become doctors.

"I recommend you stay with him while we sort out where your containers have gone." The man looks me in the eyes and waits for me to say something.

With my suitcase in one hand and the bird cage in another, I walk off the ship, down the exit, and straight onto the street.

I keep walking with no direction in mind, no sense of where I am heading, and no clue what lies ahead. No idea whether this road may lead to Saife. Or not.

CHAPTER 7

CHAUNCY

June 24, 1988

19 Chauncy Street, #18 Cambridge, Massachusetts 02138. The foreign numbers and letters Saife wrote on this torn up piece of paper stare at me. The address isn't written like my address back home. My head feels like a wasp's nest with hundreds of insects buzzing inside. I don't know the first thing about this city. I can't even speak English that well. How am I ever going to find this man or his house?

Wandering the unknown streets, my heart beats in my chest like a drum, growing louder with every passing second.

I spot a white car with a luminescent yellow light on top that reads "taxi." The taxis are white here instead of yellow like at home. This might be my only choice. I could hand over the piece of paper and ask the taxi driver to take me there. I don't have much money, and I don't know how much a taxi would cost here.

"Uh… hello," I gently greet the driver and hand him the piece of paper.

The taxi driver takes the piece of paper and stares at me for a while until he asks, "Are you Indian?" in a thick accent.

"I am Pakistani," I reply.

The man smiles and responds in Urdu, letting me know he is also from Pakistan.

"Can you take me to this address?" I ask him in Urdu.

The man's gaze lingers on me, my suitcase, and the birdcage, causing an uneasy sensation to creep up in the back of my throat. Can I trust this man? Should I have pretended to be a local? Will he take advantage of me? I contemplate stepping into the car, but I have no one else to rely on in this unfamiliar country.

Suddenly, he unbuckles his seatbelt and exits the car, revealing his towering figure and slender legs.

"Hand me the cage," he demands.

Without a second thought, I surrender the cage to him. He grasps it tightly, prompting a shrill screech from the parrot within. Circling around the front seat, he drops the steel cage onto the floor.

"Well, get in. What are you waiting for?" he calls out.

The backseat is so cramped that I struggle to bend my knees properly as I get in. A transparent plastic partition separates me from the driver, reflecting my tired eyes painted with dark purple circles. I hastily pat my overgrown hair back into place.

"Alright, are you all set for me to go?" he asks while adjusting the meter.

"Huh, oh yeah, I am all set." I feel unprepared, my hands shaking, worried about where I might be taken next. I wonder if I have enough money to pay the driver. Is this the right decision?

"Uh, when did you move here, bhai?" I ask, trying to be polite.

"I came here to start a business and get an education but never finished my studies. My parents wanted me to be a successful big man abroad. I started working and driving this taxi, and now I am addicted to the smell of dollars," he says with a chuckle.

My feet and hands stop shaking.

"What's your name, bhai?" I ask.

"Sikander," he says, looking through the rearview mirror. "But no one here can say my name; they just call me Sick. So I went from Sikander to Sick. They'll do the same to your name, don't worry. Sit back and get used to it." He makes eye contact with me through his mirror again.

As Sikander drives through the city, he points out certain buildings and street names, giving me a tour without asking.

Everything looks completely different. I have never seen so many different people—people of every race, of every color, of every shape—in one place before. My eyes wander from one face to another, captivated by the kaleidoscope of features and expressions. Some individuals have fair skin, deep blue eyes, and hair in shades of amber while others have dark complexions, almond-shaped eyes, and cascades of ebony curls. People dress to reveal more of their skin than they do at home. The colors of their clothing are a bit duller but sophisticated at times.

"But it's nice here. At first, none of the food had any flavor, even the fruit, but I like it now," Sikander says.

The streets are much wider, with cars parked on both sides of the street. In some places, the houses are all different colors, lined up in a row with a little green patch of grass in front. On other streets, massive glass buildings reach for the sky.

"We're in Cambridge now. We'll be on your street soon," Sikander says as we approach a red light.

My eyes trace the brick facades that adorn the streets, radiating warm hues. I marvel at the intricate details on the buildings and signs indicating the street names. The sunlight dances throughout the city, casting playful shadows on the trees, lights, posts, and buildings.

I roll down my window for some fresh air. As we wait for the light, I hear the melodic cadence of other languages foreign to my ears. They meld together and harmonize in the crisp summer air.

The taxi stops in front of a building that says YMCA on the left and a building with a bell tower to the right. The building reminds me of the Empress Market at home. It might have been made by a British man too. The building looks so similar to home, unlike the brick building and streets everywhere else.

We continue driving, and many churches with stained glass art appear. Many young people have backpacks and the letter "H" on their sweaters or hats. I wonder what the "H" might mean. We come to another stop as a crowd of people rush to cross the street. I peer out to the shops and notice the boxes filled with records and yellowing books in the widows.

We continue down our path, aligned with large trees and honking cars. A park toward our left seems to have a large statue inside.

"And here is your street," Sikander says, coming to a halt.

He stops in front of several brick apartments with glass doors. I try to act like I am in the right place, but I have nowhere else to go if I am not.

"Listen, Jahangir. If you ever need anything, you can call me here," Sikander says as he writes down a few digits and hands me a yellow piece of paper with a sticky top. He puts the parrot cage on the ground beside my suitcase and returns to the car.

"Sikander bhai. How much do I owe you?" I ask while tapping on his passenger-side window.

"This time, it's on me. Welcome to America. Once you've sipped this water, you won't be able to drink the water anywhere else," Sikander says and drives off.

I wasn't expecting him to decline any money from me. He could probably tell from how I am dressed in my faded jeans and a wrinkled shirt that I have little money.

I stare at the apartment again. The building is a large crimson building. The front of the apartment complex has the number nineteen. I knock on the glass door. The sound echoes throughout the neighborhood. I avoid bringing a lot of attention to myself, like a thief tiptoeing around an unfamiliar place.

Is this the right place? I hope Saife comes out of the brick building.

I walk up the steps, wrangling with the cage in one hand and my suitcase in the other. I knock on the door again.

The parrot chirps and holds on to the side of the cage with both feet. She screeches, the fear radiating off me onto her.

I open the first set of doors and step inside a small boxed enclosure with many silver rectangles along the wall with names typed from a typewriter. I try to find Saife's name or any name that sounds Pakistani to me. I search the names reading them out loud. "Jones," "Brown," "Coldwell," but do not see any familiar name. I press one of the many buttons on the wall. I wait a moment. No response. I try a few more buttons—the anticipation causing sweat to collect at my armpits. Suddenly, the door buzzes, and I pull the metal handle. The door unlocks; one of those buttons works.

I walk down the maroon-carpeted hall. The hallway reeks of cigarettes and mold. Some doors have mats outside them, and others have umbrellas leaning up against the side of the wall.

I continue walking until I see door number eighteen. Should I knock? What if it's the wrong door? I tap the white door labeled eighteen and wait for an answer. A fake money plant sits outside the door. I wait a few more seconds and knock on the door again, this time louder. My knocks reverberate through the hall.

Muffled noises buzz on the other side of the door. Sweat drips down my forehead and down my neck. I hear footsteps approaching the door. My heart beats inside my throat as if it is about to burst. The lock ticks, and the doorknob slowly turns. As my hands begin to shake, the cage shakes, unsettling the parrot.

The door opens abruptly, and I see a man shielding his face from the bright hallway. He smells of sweat and petroleum.

The man moves his hand away from his face, revealing his red eyes and scruffy beard.

"Uh, can I help you?" the man asks, rubbing his eyes. He is broadly built with large shoulders, towering over me.

"Does Saife live here?" I ask.

"Jahangir!" I hear a voice behind the man. "Jahangir, is that you? I thought I'd never see you again!" Saife rushes to the door and grabs my shoulders to embrace me.

Relief overtakes me as every muscle in my body relaxes. I release the cage and suitcase to embrace Saife.

"This is Fahad, my cousin's friend," he says.

"What are you doing here?" he asks. My father's prayers on my side must have led me to this house.

"I... I... lost my animals," I finally say, my knees weakening. I feel myself about to collapse as Saife catches me in his brawny arms.

"Don't faint here. Get your stuff. We don't have space for a tiger here anyway. Give me the bag," Saife says as he drags my body inside the house and yanks the cage and suitcase inside.

"Welcome to our home, Jahangir," Saife says as he pulls a few sheets off the yellow paisley sofa. He sits me down and brings over a cold glass of water.

"Can I stay here until I find the animals?" I ask.

"Of course, you can," Saife says.

Fahad joins us in the room and sits down on the floor.

"You'll be the fourteenth or fifteenth person here," Fahad says.

Gripping onto the parrot cage, I look at everything in the house. Wool cushions and white sheets are spread across the room.

I survey the room, taking in every detail. Something is missing here—a woman's touch. Haleema's absence is palpable, and sorrow grips my heart. I feel a slight pain, a desire, pinning throughout my chest for the sound of her gentle voice again to run my hands through her soft strands of black hair and feel the warmth of her embrace.

It looks like a place where animals live. Trash collects in every corner, the smell of bodily fluids floats through the house, the wood furniture is scratched, and the paisley sofa has silver springs sticking out of it. This house is filled with animals. Animals found in the wild. Ones that are not hand-fed food.

"In this room, it's me, Waheed, Naseem, Fahad, and now you, the fifth finger on our hand," he motions to the room closest to us. "Each room has about four or five men. Fahad stinks up the house every night." Saife laughs. He knows how ridiculous it sounds to have so many people under one roof.

"When are you going to go back to the port? And when are you going to deliver those animals to that rich snob? I mean, think of this man's audacity. He wants a tiger, and someone across the world is bringing him the tiger. What style. What class," Saife keeps talking to himself.

"I don't know where the animals are." The rush of all I lost cuts me sharper than the tiger in the cage.

"I have no idea where they are or how the ship could have lost them." I fight back the tears forming in my eyes. "They might be in the wrong truck and could be anywhere twelve hours away from here. How am I ever going to find them?" I hold my face in my hands, fighting the urge to cry.

"There's nowhere else for me to go. I have nothing with me, just this bird and this suitcase."

"Allah," Saife says with a sigh. "Now, what are you going to do?"

"What else can I do? I have to find those animals," I say with no real plan in mind.

"Get one of those cages and leave it in the woods. Whatever comes inside, take it to the rich snob," Saife laughs again.

I hide my face in my hands as tears form.

"I came here for a task and am now stuck here. The ship is going to leave in a few days. I have to get back on that boat. Otherwise, I'll be staying here with no papers, ID, or anything," I shake my head, holding back my sobs.

"So you think I have any of that?" Saife says. "The animals will show up. Someone will get the container, and their skin will jump off their body when they open it to see a tiger and birds by the hundreds. They'll contact the ship and let you know. You'll get back on that boat."

Maybe Saife is right. The containers will end up in the wrong location, and someone must inform the ship. I will go wherever they say the animals are and bring them to their new owners.

"For now, you can sleep where you find space here. Treat it like the zoo," Saife says as he winks and enters the kitchen. "We have a few rules in this house," Fahad says. "If you see a bed or place to sleep, then sleep. If you see food in the fridge, then eat. Rent is due on the first of every month. If anyone asks where you live, do not tell them you live here. We only have three rooms, and there are fifteen of us now, including you. You will meet a different member of the house depending on the time of day," Fahad recites the rules.

I check on the parrot, who is staring back at me. "This is going to be our home for now," I whisper to the parrot. She does not seem amused or impressed with her new home. At least it's not surrounded by miles of sea.

I trail after Saife as he heads to the kitchen, my nose wrinkling in disgust at the foul odor emanating from the sink drain. To calm my queasy stomach, I splash cold water on my face and run my hands through my hair before following Saife back to the living room.

But the sight only makes things worse. The paisley sofa is buried under a heap of stained sheets, pillows, and cushions, creating a cluttered mess. It's a wonder anyone can even walk around in this house.

"Everyone here works around the clock," Saife says while moving some cushions around the common area. "You won't see some of us for more than twenty-four hours. We nap at the parking lots or behind the counter at the convenience store. We know our next shift will start before we can make it home, so we end up sleeping in each other's cars or during their shifts."

"And we all take turns cooking here. I'll let you know when it's your turn. But you might be gone by then. We buy groceries from the outdoor market in huge bulk. One of us makes food each day to last the entire day," Saife continues while widening his hand to gesture a lot of food or a large pot.

Luckily for them, I won't stick around long enough to cook a meal. Cooking has never been my forte, and I have no desire to poison anyone with my lack of culinary skills.

"Anyway, you must be tired, Jahangir. Why don't you go freshen up in the bathroom, and I'll clear some of the sofa for you to sleep here with me? I'll leave in a few hours so you can take the rest of the space," he says as he fluffs the pillows.

Saife talks nonstop about the other people living in the apartment. He continues talking as I tune him out and sink into the cushions.

Moments later, Saife is snoring with his mouth wide open. As I bury my face in the stain-filled sofa, a flood of emotions run through my body. I am exhausted from losing my animals yet grateful to have met Saife and have a place to rest my head for a few days until I find them. In just a few days, I will be reunited with all of them.

My eyes droop slowly, and I feel the thoughts in my mind slow down. I think about my family, about Haleema. Her soft velvety skin. I want to embrace her and cover her in my kisses.

Someone will find my animals by tomorrow.

CHAPTER 8

CAGE

———

June 25, 1988

Everywhere I look, shades and hues stretch as far as the eye can see.

Clusters of purple and green grapes glisten while pomegranates, defying their seasonal limitations, sit proudly in open crates. Bananas, so large and plump, are stacked together along with vibrant peppers in shades of red, green, and yellow. Alongside them, carrots in vivid orange and cauliflower in pristine white beckon. I marvel at the seemingly endless variety of fruits and vegetables, each carefully packaged in tightly sealed boxes. It feels as if this place holds enough food to nourish the entire nation.

Saife mentioned a small store to buy anything I might need for my week-long stay. But I hadn't anticipated the numerous choices.

No vendors or sellers push their carts here. We are entirely indoors, where food resides in freezers and fridges. No one interacts with each other. There is no haggling over prices. People have their carts or small baskets and walk through the orderly aisles.

As I walk throughout the building, my eyes scan the rows of aisles, attempting to decipher the labels. Cooking has always been a foreign concept to me, and now I find myself responsible for preparing food for everyone while adhering to the house rules. Saife informed me that we typically shop together and divide the groceries, but I decide to buy a few items on my own just in case.

As I wander through the store, a rumble in my stomach sends vibrations through my body, reminding me of the comforting meals Mama used to prepare. I yearn for the warmth of freshly made roti and the tantalizing sensations that danced on my tongue.

While navigating the aisles, I come across a few bags of sunflower seeds, which I buy for the parrot. Uncertain if I can find proper bird feed elsewhere at the moment, I realize that in a few days, I will be leaving Saife's house and embarking on a journey to deliver the animals.

With my limited selection in hand, I make my way toward the checkout line, joining the orderly queue of people patiently waiting to purchase their groceries. Unlike the chaos and jostling back home, the line here is organized, with individuals respecting one another's space—nothing like home.

After checking out, I carry my bags and exit the store. Walking back to Saife's apartment, I hear the loud noises of cars as life goes on around me.

A peculiar heaviness weighs upon the door, making it more arduous to open than before. A medley of clamorous noises floods my ears from within, resembling the uproar of a bustling circus. Boisterous shouts and screams echo in the room by the voices of men.

"Try to catch it!" I hear someone urgently yell as I step inside.

"The bird is loose!" Comes another voice, filled with alarm.

"Why on Earth did you open the cage, you idiot!" bellows a deep, frustrated tone.

Are they talking about my parrot? In my haste, my bags slip from my grasp and collide with the floor, their contents scattering in disarray. Ignoring the chaos of spilled groceries, I hurry into the room, my heart pounding. The once-secure gate of the birdcage now stands ajar with no trace of my feathery companion within its confines.

"Jahangir, I didn't think the bird would fly out," the curly haired man shouts. His coils bounce as he runs after the parrot.

"It's a bird! Of course, it will fly out!" I scream.

The bird flaps its wings. Her gray feathers and red tail catch everyone's eyes in the room. Majestically the bird flies around the room.

"I just thought she looked sad in her cage. I wanted to let her fly for a little bit. It's a bird. She shouldn't be caged up. She was starting to remind me of us. All caged up in this place, unable to fly and live freely."

"The bird is for a customer. It's not my pet. I need to get it back into the cage," I say, realizing I will never be able to get the parrot's attention. How will I be able to get her back into her cage? Something that doesn't want to be contained. That doesn't want to be bothered.

"I thought it was yours," the man says.

"Why would I bring a pet parrot to America?" I ask, irritated.

The parrot eventually settles atop the bookshelf, perched at a height that requires a chair. Without wasting a moment,

I rush toward the bookshelf, grasping a chair along the way, determined to retrieve her. As I reach out from behind, she let out piercing screeches and cries, clawing at my hands and sinking her sharp beak into my tightly clenched fingers.

"You won't escape again," I whisper sternly to the parrot before placing her back inside the cage. She bites at the cage, trying to open it and set herself free. I turn to the man I was speaking with.

"Do not ever touch the parrot again," I warn, my voice tingles with frustration.

"I just thought she wanted to be out," he replies defensively.

"Don't try that again," I sigh wearily. "It won't happen again. In just a few days, I'll leave this place for good. I'll return to the port and find my animals. You won't have to deal with us anymore."

Anger wells up within me, wanting to lash out my frustration toward this man. Slowly returning to the spilled groceries, I retrieve a packet of seeds and pour a portion into a container for the parrot.

Meanwhile, the man lingers in the living room area, sitting on one of the scattered mattresses. I realize I have not seen him before, yet he knows my name.

"What is your name?" I inquire, attempting to forget him taking my parrot out of the cage.

"Waheed," he replies, extending his hand. "Look, Jahangir, I didn't mean to upset you." Sweat glistens on his forehead. "My cousin, Saife, said you worked at some sorta zoo and brought animals. He said you're from Karachi. I just got excited seeing the parrot and wanted to pet her. I didn't think she would be this hard to get back into the cage."

"It's fine. Just make sure never to do it again," I respond, attempting to soothe my anger. "And make sure the rest of this circus knows not to touch it. The parrot and I will be out of here in no time."

After our conversation, I remember that Waheed is here to become a doctor. Saife mentioned his cousin has a master's degree from a university in Lahore and came here to become a doctor. He drives a taxi during the day, works at the gas station at night, and studies.

"Where is Saife?" I ask.

"He's working at the gas station," Waheed says.

"Okay, well, I will see you later, Waheed. I am leaving my parrot here. Do not touch her," I say as I head back out the door.

I slip out of the house and walk toward the port. The phone number of the landline for the apartment is scrawled in my pocket, a lifeline that I cling to as I navigate the unfamiliar street.

With a map in hand, I set out on foot, determined to get an update on my animals. I follow the winding streets, taking care to avoid the highways that stretch out like veins across the city. As I walk, I hear the distant hum of traffic.

Mile after mile, I trudge on, feeling exhausted with fear settling heavily in my bones. But I carry on, driven by the smell of the ocean. I must be nearby.

Finally, the sight of hundreds, maybe even thousands, of containers resting at a port with a massive ship docked beside it looms before me. Red, blue, maroon, white, and gray containers are stacked one on the other. I am sure they must have found my container. I make my way through the location, trying to find someone to speak to.

The port feels as if it goes on for acres. The sounds of alarms and moving trucks fill my ears. Directional signs are posted around the port, and massive machinery carries containers.

Who should I speak to? I approach one of the men giving people directions.

"Excuse me," I say, but I am unable to capture his attention.

"Excuse me," I say louder.

"What! Don't you see us doing something here? Get back on the ship you came from," he shouts.

"I want to, but I lost my animals, I mean container," I try to explain.

"Go over to that building." The man points at a lighthouse-shaped building with several windows. "They will have the information of every container."

I walk over, avoiding the large puddles of water collecting on the ground.

I tap the glass window, not seeing any doors or a way to walk inside. A man appears at the window. He has a thick yellow mustache and a red face covered in brown spots. His eyes are a bright blue, the same shade as a cloudless sky.

"I am looking for my container. My name is Jahangir. I was here yesterday," I shout over the loud beeping sounds of the trucks backing up.

"You have the container number?" The man shouts back.

"Yes, I do." I hand him the piece of paper with the container number.

He shuts the window and disappears. I don't know what to expect or do. I wait a few minutes; a few minutes turn into a half hour, a half-hour into an hour, until finally, the man appears in front of me at the window.

"Jahangir. We can't seem to find your container location," the man with the yellow mustache says.

Where could the animals have gone? How can they still be missing? My heart races as sweat drips down my back. "Where has it gone? The animals in those containers can't live for very long. They need food. They can't be in their cages for too long," I lose my breath as my head spins. "We don't know where they are. But you can leave your number here, and if anything changes, we'll call you and let you know the location. No one has reported having found animals," the man says.

Defeated, I head back to the apartment. My feet feel like cinder blocks as I drag myself back to the last place I want to be.

It's nearly dark out when I arrive at the apartment. The streetlights illuminate the park by the apartment. Barely any cars pass by the deserted streets.

I walk inside and check on the parrot. She hasn't eaten any of the seeds.

"Yar, Jahangir, where have you been?" Saife's voice approaches me from the other room. The other housemates have left for their night shifts at the various gas stations, convenience stores, or parking lots.

"I heard your parrot was flying around here." Saife laughs, but I am in no mood to laugh. I can't do anything right now.

"Saife, I don't think I am ever going to find those animals," I tell him. Tears pour down my face.

"No, yar. We will find them. Did you go back to the port today?" Saife asks.

Overwhelmed with despair, I recount the news to Saife, my voice trembling with sadness. "I was just there, and they don't have the animals. They don't know where the animals are. It can be days or weeks until they can find them. There is nothing I can do. I need to find a way to call Salim bhai. I need to tell him the customer won't get the animals," I say as tears stream down my face like a waterfall.

"We can call him!" Saife exclaims. "Let me gather some quarters and call from the nearest payphone. International calls can be expensive, but we can manage it. Do you have Salim bhai's number?"

I nod my head aggressively. Together, we hurry out of the room and descend the stairs, venturing to the pay phone. The darkness blankets our surroundings, but the streets come alive with vibrant lights as people throng shops and restaurants. I catch whiffs of unfamiliar aromas mixed with spices and barbecue. Several illuminated signs cast a colorful glow onto the sidewalk. The park nearby is empty, with only a few rodents scurrying around.

As we approached the payphone, beneath the flickering glow of a lamppost, it becomes a beacon of hope. Its faded metal exterior bears the scars of time and countless users.

Saife dials several numbers, engaging in multiple conversations over the phone. The scent of lingering cigarette smoke permeates the air around the pay phone. Shattered fragments of glass scatter the ground.

Saife persists, requesting to speak to Salim bhai. On the other end of the line, I could hear the familiar cadence of Urdu. Saife places the receiver against my ear. Taking a deep breath, I greet the voice on the other end, "Asalam Alaykum."

"Walikum Asalam," I hear Salim bhai's voice resonate on the other end, a mix of warmth and concern. What if he is upset? He is an understanding man. Memories resurface, like whispers from my childhood when several bird cages were stolen from our zoo in the dead of night. He had brushed it off, attributing it to the divine plan of Allah.

"Salim bhai, it's me, Jahangir," I utter, the phone cord coiling around my body as I attempt to communicate amid the clamor of the streets. Honks and car noises filled the air, blending with the bustling sounds of lovers strolling arm in arm along the sidewalks. Teenagers parade by, their radios blaring loud music.

"Jahangir! How are you? Have you reached America? Are the animals safely delivered? We all have been praying for your safety," Salim bhai asks as my palms grow clammy, the phone slipping from my grasp. What is he going to do when I say the animals are lost? Will he be understanding again, or will he have me indebted to him? Or worse, would he track down my relatives, subjecting them to unforeseen consequences? No, Salim bhai is a good man. He would never bring harm to my family.

"Salim bhai, I don't have much time, but I wanted to tell you that I have something bad to say..."

"Hurry up, Jahangir. International calls cost a lot. I will run out of money soon," Saife slaps the back of my neck while inserting another quarter through the slit on the phone.

"I don't have the animals. The port lost them. I was feeding them for months, and now there is no sign of them ever being with me," I blurt out. The line is silent.

"Hello?" I ask.

"Jahangir, if this is what Allah had in mind, this is what will happen. Try to stay there for a few more weeks and see if you can find them. Otherwise, we will figure it out when we see you back," Salim bhai says calmly. I know this is a huge financial loss for him, but he doesn't sound worried.

"Okay, Salim bhai. I will get going," I say.

"Jahangir, you will be able to find the animals. Do not worry. Allah Hafiz." The line cuts off. A loud beeping sound echoes as I put the phone down.

"What happened?" Saife asks frantically.

"He wasn't mad. He said these things are up to Allah," I say without realizing the words are leaving my mouth. My mind is thinking about what's next.

I need to stay here longer. It's only a matter of a few days or even weeks. I could earn some extra money working with Saife.

"Saife, can you get me a job with you?" I find the words leaving my mouth without even thinking.

"A job?" he utters in disbelief. "Of course. Your English is so good. They will keep you at the store. And if you know how to drive, you can take Waheed's taxi around too. Why don't you come to the Green Street Garage, and I can ask the manager if he can give you a job there," Saife says.

"Can we go to the garage tomorrow? I'll work anywhere. The garage, taxi, or gas station," I say eagerly. I want to save time lounging around in the city. If I can earn a few extra dollars, I will.

"You'll get addicted to the crinkling sound of paper bills," Saife says jokingly.

I can do nothing else for now. I will have to stay here longer than I wanted. I have already been away for so long on the ship and will need to start working to send my family money back home. My youngest sister, Goodi, still needs to get married, an expense I will endure. If I earn a lot, who knows, maybe like Saife, I won't return home.

CHAPTER 9

LETTER

—

September 6, 1988

A familiar feeling dwells on me as I enter through the front door. It feels like someone from my home is here to visit. As if by twisting the golden handle of the door, I will find Papa sitting on the gray stain-filled sofa, waiting to embrace me. But I am wrong.

When Fahad and I returned home from another long dreary day working at the gas station, I find no one waiting for me. My gut tells me that a piece of home is lingering somewhere here. The smell of warmth, of love, of Karachi fills the room.

"Jay, there's mail for you today too. It looks like someone finally remembered you are alive," Fahad jokes as he passes me an envelope.

"I mean, it's just been several months since you've been here, and your family finally sent you a sign that they know you exist," Fahad teases me as he lies on the couch. He places his feet on the scratched coffee table and shuffles through his pockets until he finds a lighter for his cigarette.

The thick envelope weighs down on my callused fingertips. Many stamps stuck to the top right corner of the envelope, marking several countries and people it must have passed through before getting to me.

Who might have sent this to me? The thick stamps and postage at the top make it seem like it came from Pakistan. The letter is addressed to me, but the handwriting isn't recognizable. I only told Papa the address of this place, expecting him not to remember or understand how to interpret it. Someone from my family must have brought the letter to the post office and told the clerk the address.

I open the letter, careful not to rip and tear it too much. The top is sealed with tape and glue. White-lined pieces of paper slip out of the envelope onto the coffee-stained table. Slowly, I unfold one of the pieces of paper written in Urdu. It's Papa's handwriting.

My eyes fixate on the letters and words. I've yearned to see the curves and dots of my mother tongue. It has been months since I've seen these letters or read Papa's handwriting. The papers smell of home, the same smell lingering through my head when I returned home.

Homes possess a unique scent, an essence that silently permeates every corner. I had never truly grasped this until I arrived in this foreign abode. The apartment reeks of sweat and gasoline, a testament to the toil and sweat we men endure in our daily grind. The grime and dirt of our labor cling to us, just as the animals in a zoo carry their distinctive odors.

Yet these papers exude an entirely different fragrance— an aroma reminiscent of jasmine or honey, something else floral and earthy.

My eyes focus on the lined sheets in my hands. The handwriting is crisp but difficult for me to read. Papa tends to leave certain letters un-dotted, confusing me further.

"Fahad, can you come over here," I ask as I organize the pages in order. "Can you read this letter from my father? I never was good at reading Urdu."

"You can't read Urdu?" Fahad says with fascination.

"I can read it, but it's hard to read my father's writing."

"Here I go," Fahad clears his throat and holds the letter in both of his hands as if he is about to give an important speech. "Raja." Fahad pauses and stares. "Who's Raja?"

"Raja is my name at home." I shrug my shoulders. "My wife is the only person who doesn't call me Raja. She is stubborn, but that's why I married her. Regardless, anyone I love more than life itself calls me Raja."

"Well, don't expect me to start calling you Raja." Fahad laughs.

"I'm not asking you to call me Raja," I roar. "Will you read my letter already? I'm dying to know how my father is doing." Heat rises in my face.

"Raja. It says, 'The smell of the rain reminds me of how you would dance in the puddles with Siraj and Rizwan during the monsoon season. We would run after you begging you not to step outside as the gutters overflowed with dirty water onto the streets. The ceiling caved in a bit from the storm, but I fixed it once it stopped raining.'"

Fahad's voice fades as he reads the letter, mumbling under his breath. He may be struggling to read the handwriting. When he stops altogether, I stare at him. He is quiet. I hear someone in another room snoring while my parrot cracks a seed open. Fahad looks up at me from the papers, his eyes swell.

"I can't keep reading this letter," Fahad says. "Your father misses you, Jahangir. You should go back. Forget the fucking animals. He needs you, and so does your family," Fahad says as he puts the pieces of paper on the wooden table.

"I wasn't there when my father died," he chokes out. "I was stuck here with no papers. If I left, there wouldn't be a way for me to get back. It will always be my biggest regret in life. I won't ever hear my father tell me he's proud of me. I won't be able to hear the sound of his voice again. There will never be a chance for him to tell me he is proud of the man I become. You don't have to live with that guilt." Tears streaming down his face.

"Forget the fucking animals, Jay. Go back home." Fahad wipes away the tears from his face.

I gather the pieces of paper as Fahad walks away, slamming the front door behind him as he scurries off. The smell of the lit cigarette fills the air, leaving a trail of smoke as it rests in the ashtray.

Holding the white-lined papers, I struggle to make out the words. The words that traveled thousands of miles remind me that my father is still alive, unlike Fahad's father.

I flatten out the paper and try to make out the words.

Raja,   *July 20, 1988*
My ears yearn for the sound of your voice.

The smell of the rain reminds me of how you would dance in the puddles with Siraj and Rizwan during the monsoon season. We would run after you begging you not to step outside as the gutters overflowed with dirty water onto the streets. The ceiling caved in a bit from the storm, but I fixed it once it stopped raining. Your mother couldn't stand the sounds of the drops collecting in the buckets. I found it rather peaceful knowing the droplets could be used to water the garden. We ate your favorite lentils with rice after the storm. Your mother is such an excellent cook. I sometimes want to lick the plate after licking my fingers clean.

Ramzan is quickly approaching. Do not forget to pray and wake up for Fajr. Your mother won't be there to wake you up with paratha and chai. Ramzan won't be the same without you. You would drag your brothers and the rest of the boys in the neighborhood to tarabeeh with you every night. Who will drag them by the ear and take them to the masjid now? What I will miss the most is you sitting next to me during iftar. I still leave your spot open when we sit down to eat. I point at the seat and let everyone know you'll join us for the meal. You still join us in my heart. Siraj jokes that he will eat your portion of the meal, too, if you don't join us, and he doesn't fail every night.

Beta, as you know, I am growing old and do not know how many more days I have left in this world. Every day I think it is my last day. I wake up grateful to see another day, another chance at seeing you and hoping to hold you close to me again. To be able to hear the beat of your heart against mine. Another day to tell you to cut your hair. Another day to tell you how proud of you I am.

Your sister, Goodi, is getting married soon. She is busy picking out her lavish clothes and jewelry. I went and booked the hall you suggested in Nazimabad. They were asking for an arm and leg, but I told them I was your father, and they lowered the price. It was the same man who was there when we had your Valima. He said he remembered you handing out food to all the workers and the people outside the hall. No matter what happens, please attend your youngest sister's wedding. We are all waiting for your arrival, beta. Anytime someone knocks three times on the door, my heart races, anticipating it will be you peering behind, ready to jump out.

For the first few moments of my day, I lie in bed thinking if I was a good father to you. I gave you nothing; you gave your family more than we could have imagined. You have been more of a father to your siblings than I have. The money you sent for their education, the money you sent for Mama's medicine. The money you sent us ensures we have an AC, a generator, and running water.

Every time I go to the bank and pass the paper bills through the window, I think about how I am giving the banker my son in exchange. I'd rather you be here than this money. My eyes hurt as I think about how I have sold my son. Raja, I want to have you here with us again. Try to understand the pain I must feel to have an extension of my heart thousands of miles away without asking him if he is okay.

There is a saying in Urdu when kids ask their parents which kid they love the most. I know you have heard me say plenty of times that parents never have a favorite child. We all have five fingers on our hands; it won't matter to the hand which one you cut. Each finger will hurt the same. If you represented a finger on my hand, that finger would hurt the most if cut. Why is the one that would hurt the most the furthest from me?

Please don't make me wait longer than I need. My eyelids get heavy thinking about how far you are, where you might be, what you might be eating, where you might be sleeping.

I am very proud to call you my son. My strongest and bravest son.

May Allah bless you with all good fortune and prosperity. I will say your name in every prayer.

Your father

CHAPTER 10

MATCH

October 26, 1988

Yet another day, I am defeated. I walk back home from the port to see if my animals were found. The sounds of the machines unloading and beeping still ring in my ears. Where could these animals be? It's been months. Surely, someone would have found these containers full of animals in the wrong place. I am giving up on the hope that I will ever be able to find them.

Donned in a plaid jacket I bought at the Salvation Army, I board the red line train to Harvard Station. Stepping off at the station, I walk the crimson brick-covered streets to Chauncy Street. Autumn brings forth a chill in the air. Wind gusts, shaking the red, yellow, and orange leaves off the tree and sending a shiver through my entire being. The trees are turning a bright auburn. The town looks as if it is up in flames.

Arriving at the entrance of our apartment, I catch a glimpse of my reflection in the glass front door, an unyielding witness to my return. Yet another day, I find myself here, grappling with unanswered questions from my family's letter about when I will be home. I pass the row of silver mailboxes being dutifully replenished and step through our apartment door. I twist the gold handle and walk in.

The gray parrot sings as the door slams behind me. Her fluffy feathers crunch at the top of her neck as she sees me arrive. I walk over to her cage and see she only has a few drops of water and little seeds left. I unlock the cage to take the water holder and feeder out. As I take the containers to the kitchen to rinse them out, I hear someone rush out of the bathroom door.

"It's almost time!" Saife yells while running into the room. His voice bounces along the empty walls of our home. "The Pakistan and India match is on. It's happening now in Lahore!" He's beating his chest as he says Lahore.

"I am trying," Naseem says, looking behind the TV and adjusting the various wires. "I forget what the guy said about getting international TV. He said there's a way to steal it."

The last time I watched a match was back home with my brothers. There's no one on the road for miles in my neighborhood if Pakistan and India are playing against each other. Even during prayer times, the imam will recite the shortest verses, ensuring our prompt return to watch the match.

Naseem finagles with the antennas and wires and turns the knobs on the TV. I wash out the holders and fill one up with seeds. They hit the plastic holder, sounding like rain falling and reminding me of my morning tasks at Al-Ahmed Animal House.

"Hurry up, Naseem!" Saife says, jumping up and down while shaking the entire coach.

Cricket is a way of life, a religion, back home. I remember coming home from primary school to join the boys in the neighborhood for matches. We'd set up sticks as wickets and take turns teaching each other how to spin the ball when pitching to each other. We all wanted to be good enough to play for the Pakistan team. Everyone's dream was to be able to represent our country on the international level.

The static of the TV continues until we hear the announcer read the score and slowly see the cricket field appear on the TV. The Pakistani team is batting while India is fielding. It's the last day of the match.

"Yar, turn the volume up. I can't hear a thing," Saife says with his hands on his head, already sweating with anxiety without knowing the score.

"I've never watched an entire match," Naseem says.

"Sit down. I'll explain it," I tell Naseem. "It's pretty simple. One team will bat, and the other team will field." I point at the TV to indicate which team is holding the bat and show the men on the field.

"The batting team will send two batters at a time, one on each end of the wickets." I point at the wickets on either end of the rectangle on the screen. "The batsmen will hit the ball and run to the other wicket to get a run, which is one point. The batsman can also hit the ball to the boundary and get four points, a choka, or outside the boundary and get six points, a chaka. The batter's job is to hit the ball to defend the wickets." I pause to see if he is following along.

"You don't want the bowler to hit the wicket. Those sticks on either side where you see the batsman standing in front of," I explain while imitating throwing a fastball.

"If the bowler hits the wicket, you are out, and the batting team will send another batter until there are ten outs," Saife says, putting up ten fingers with his hands. "The fielding team can get you out in many ways. The baller can hit the wickets behind the batsman, anyone on the fielding team can catch the ball, or a fielder can hit the wickets when the batsmen are running to get the point."

"There are many other rules, but I'll explain them if they come up. Does that make sense, Naseem?" I ask.

"I get it." Naseem nods. "I was always confused why there were two batters at a time. Now I understand you can hit it and run to the other side. I never watched enough to understand fully. We didn't have a TV, and the radio didn't make it easier to follow," Naseem says.

I'm surprised to know Naseem hasn't watched much cricket before. Every man I know loves cricket. It is what makes us men. It's a religious practice for us. We play alongside the other boys in our alleyways, pausing only to let cars pass. During Ramzan, we play at night after eating. Cricket is in our blood; it runs through our veins.

Naseem is a provider, more than the rest of us. Dark violet circles form under his eyes from working every midnight shift at the Green Street Garage. His family relies on him to send money. He is their only option—the breadwinner.

"Out!" Saife screams as he claps his hands. "That is our captain! He is the best player Pakistan has ever seen." Saife dances, moving his shoulders up and down with his hands in the air.

"He might be the most dedicated player in the league," I join in.

That's the key to many good players—their work ethic. I look at Naseem, who works over a hundred hours a week. He has the weight of his family over his shoulders like the rest of us do, but he handles the stress gracefully. And then there's the captain, with the weight of Pakistan on his shoulders.

"Watching the game at home has its fun," Saife says with his eyes still glued to the TV. "All of us brothers and sisters would gather around and watch over one tiny screen. We would scream and shout together. You see people hanging the green flag with the white crescent and star outside their balconies. We'd take turns praying in the other room for our team."

It really isn't the same watching the match here, but we are all still together, watching one way or another. I imagine my family gathering with tea and salty snacks to watch the match right now too.

I put my arms over Saife's broad, wide shoulders and bring him closer to me.

"We are all brothers here watching together," I tell him. He yanks my shirt a bit in a playful tease, and I pat his back a little.

Whether or not we have known each other for very long, we are all brothers under this roof and take care of each other together.

"Let's go play a few rounds now," I say, getting up.

"There's no place to play here," Saife utters.

"We could play right on the street," Naseem suggests.

"They'll call the police on us, and then what are we going to do," Saife exclaims.

"Nothing like that will happen. Come on. Let's go," I say as I shake the others awake.

"Let's go play cricket," I burst out in excitement.

Saife finds a ball and a piece of wood from the cabinet shelf. The wood can act as a bat for now. We gather on the street and take turns bowling and batting. Screaming and swearing at each other while being careful not to hit a parked car or anyone walking by.

For the first time in many months, I am reminded of home. The sound of the ball hitting the bat and the shouting among all of us.

After an hour of playing, we all slow down. "Alright, I think we had a fun match," Saife says, huffing with his hands on his knees and bent over while sweat races down his face. The sun's rays dance along his face as he wipes off the sweat.

"That was a good match. I'm ready for a shower," I say as I run my hand through Saife's wet hair.

We walk inside the house, and Naseem places the plank of wood against the wall in the kitchen. The sun lights up the room, leaving an orange glow. The gray parrot sings as she hears the door slam behind us shut.

Saife runs past me to the bathroom to shower first before anyone else comes home for the evening.

Naseem pulls the wobbly white chair from the table and sits. I search for the rusted kettle from the cabinet and run some water until it's half full. I grab a few packets of black tea, crush a few cloves, pieces of cardamom, and cinnamon sticks in my hand, and toss them in the water.

"Today was fun. Thanks, Jay, for teaching me," Naseem says.

"Now, when you go home, you can teach everyone else, too," I say while stirring the tea.

"Home," Naseem says with his voice trailing off. "This is home now. I don't plan to go back."

"Why?" I ask.

"How do I explain? There's nothing for me back home. What I can do here and send back to my family is incomparable to what I made at home. You know what I mean? Did you earn this much from collecting tickets at the lot or filling up someone's gas?" Naseem asks.

I shake my head. He is right; I couldn't provide as much from my salary at Al-Ahmed Animal House.

"Exactly. Jay, what's your plan?" Naseem asks. I watch the water boil, turning from clear to brown.

"My plan for what?" I ask, buying a few more seconds before answering.

"You came here for some animals. It has been months, and they are nowhere to be found. Why are you still here?" he asks.

"If I go back, I won't be able to give this much to my family. If I leave, I don't know how I will come back. I don't have papers," I say while pouring a little milk into the kettle. Bubbles form in the pot.

"You can get papers. I'm trying to do the same thing and might marry someone here for the paper," Naseem says.

"I can't do that. I already have a wife," I utter, looking away. My sweat from earlier stings my eyes.

"No one knows that here," Naseem says. "Once I have papers, I will bring my entire family here. My brothers, sisters, and parents. You should do the same."

Saife rushes out of the shower covered in a beige towel with strings falling apart at the end. He pushes past me, running to the hot milk chai.

"Today has been fun," Saife says, sipping the tea and making loud slurping sounds.

"Think about it. It won't get better for people like us at home. This is it for us," Naseem says, picking the towel off Saife's shoulder and entering the bathroom.

"What was he blabbering about?" Saife asks, adding a heaping spoonful of sugar to his tea. The steam leaves the cup as he stirs.

"Nothing. How's the tea?" I ask.

Saife's mouth moves, but I block out the sounds of his voice. How else am I going to stay? Is this the only route left for me? An uneasy feeling forms in my chest.

I take a sip of tea from my mug. It burns my tongue.

I feel nauseated at the thought of marrying another woman just to be able to stay here. What other choice do I have left? My chest tightens.

CHAPTER 11

VCR

———

November 24, 1988

Waheed arrives home, pride dripping from the curls on his head. He beams joyfully as he holds on to a cardboard box wrapped in silver duct tape from top to bottom. His veins are prominent on his arms as he struggles to lift the box to rest on the table, releasing a sigh of relief.

Something extraordinary resides within that box. Waheed would not look this happy otherwise. I inch closer to the box to see what he bought.

My interest piques as I inch closer to the box. Through the duct tape, I manage to decipher the letters written on the side. V-C-R.

"You got us a VCR! How did you get so much money to—" Waheed yanks the box closer to himself.

"Don't touch the box!" He hits my hand, reaching out.

"My father will be the first to open and use the box. When I return home at the semester's end, I'll gift it to him. I can't wait to see the look on his face," Waheed says as his voice echoes in the kitchen.

"His son brought him back a VCR set. He is going to be so happy," Waheed says while rubbing the sides of the box as if a genie will come out and grant him three more wishes.

"That's not for another month. And you don't even know if you'll get a green card. We're all waiting for our papers to process. It could take more than a year. At least we can use it 'til you go back home," I insist.

"Did I buy it with your money?" he asks. "Then no." Waheed smirks.

"Oh, come on. Don't be like that," I say.

The door opens and slams closed as Saife returns from his night shift at the gas station. I can smell his arrival; the strong scent of gasoline lingers with him. It stays on all of us when we leave the gas station.

Saife's eyes fall on the VCR immediately. "Yar, Waheed, did you finally win the lottery? Where did you get this new VCR set?" He reaches for the box.

"Don't touch the box," Waheed says as he slaps Saife's hands.

"I'm not about to eat the VCR set." Saife chuckles. "Let us see the VCR and test it out."

"I already tested it out, so don't ruin this gift for my father. If in six more months I save enough, I will get one for my sister's dowry for her wedding. I want them all to know they have a brother here in America," Waheed continues talking as he drags a chair from the living room into the kitchen, placing it along the counter as a stepping stool.

Waheed lifts the box, his muscles strain, and his shoulders collapse.

"How much does that weigh? You can't pick it up. You won't be able to put it up there on the cabinet," I say.

"And even if you do, I am still going to open it in the middle of the night and plug it in and watch that new James Bond movie with Jahangir," Saife says, letting out a loud cackle. "Fine, if you sisterfuckers want to see the VCR so badly, I will open it, and we can watch one movie and only one movie, and then do not ask to use the VCR no matter what," Waheed says with fury.

He rips the duct tape at the top of the box, peeling it back and taking some of the cardboard. He pulls the box's flaps and throws the crumbled newspaper on the floor, revealing what is inside.

My mouth falls open, and my eyes widen.

"Waheed, what did you buy?" I say, bringing my hands closer to my face to hide my wide mouth.

Saife wipes his eyes and moves his face closer to the box.

Inside the box wrapped in layers and layers of duct tape, we see dark round black circular objects. Rocks.

"Ya, Allah! Waheed, this is the shit you wouldn't let us touch?" Saife and I laugh hysterically. My heart races.

Waheed holds his head in both of his hands and turns red. "That bastard at the pawn store showed me the VCR and tested it out and wrapped it in front of me," he says as he rips the pieces of newspaper left in the box. His hands shuffle through the box of rocks, searching for the VCR set.

The sound of laughter floods the room as the other men walk into the living room to see what the noise is all about.

Saife is on the floor laughing and holding his stomach. He mockingly says, "No, Saife, don't touch the box. My father will watch the new movies on this."

I slap his hand. "When I have enough money, I will get my sister one for her wedding. Yar, she would take these rocks out of the box and throw them at your head," I say as

Waheed grabs two rocks in his hands and throws them at us. The rocks hit the side of my stomach. I laugh even more.

I help Saife off the floor. He takes one of the rocks from the box and hands it to Waheed. "Let me know how that new James Bond movie is." Saife yanks at the back of Waheed's neck.

Waheed starts to tremble. Both of his hands catch his falling head as he slumps and falls on the chair he was going to use as a stepping stool. In between his fingers, his face appears crimson.

"This country just continues to give us rocks. I spent months saving that money to give my father something special, and I got a box of rocks," he says in between sobs.

Tears run down his face, leaving wet marks on his shirt.

"I was just trying to do something for my father." He sighs.

"This isn't anything to cry about." Saife rushes over to Waheed.

"Look, you managed to buy this once; I will help you buy one again for *chacha*—uncle." Saife rests Waheed's face on his stomach and gently rubs his face, hushing him.

I throw the rocks and newspaper back in the box. The duct tape is still sticky. I reassemble the flaps and pat the duct tape along the seams.

"It's okay. You just need to focus on your studies. When you're a doctor, chacha will have a shiny new VCR set in every room." Saife coddles Waheed's head and wipes away his tears.

All these hours of hard work just to save up for something luxurious but wasted on some rocks. This December, he would have gone home for the first time in years. He wanted to come back with something nice. I understand that feeling. I have stayed for the same reason.

Sometimes I wonder if I would have stayed even if I had delivered the animals. Would I have gotten used to how much I could send home? These long hours of laborious work lead to a few moments of pleasure for my family.

"Come on now. Get up." Saife wraps his arms around Waheed, enclosing him to his chest and pushing him out of the seat.

"Jay, can you warm up some okra and roti from last night," Saife says as he points at the fridge.

"Just eat a little. It will lighten up your mood." Saife rests his head on top of Waheed's head, pressing the curls.

I walk over to the fridge and find the cold silver handles of the pot filled with food. It's still heavy with a lot left over from last night.

I uncover the lid to find okra inside. It's gooey and mushy. No food here has the taste of a woman's touch.

I place the pot on the stove. The room smells of spices, reminding me of home, of Haleema. She used to make the best okra I ever ate. This won't satisfy my taste buds.

Saife places two more chairs by the dining table. The chair wobbles as Saife sits down.

The okra sizzles in the pot. It's warm enough to eat. I plop some of the gooey mess of green stems and yellowish-pale seeds on white plates.

"Here, Waheed. This will make you feel better." I slide the plate in front of him. "Don't worry too much now. Everything will be fine," I say as I pat his head.

"Who made this shit?" Waheed says, letting out a small smile.

"It was Fahad's first time making okra. He didn't know that you shouldn't wash it after you cut it," I say while sliding my chair closer to the table.

"However, it is. Just eat it," Saife says, leaning into Waheed with his arm around the back of Waheed's neck.

"Us being here is for survival," Waheed says as he grabs some of the okra with his hands.

"Allah. This is really bad," Waheed says while laughing. We all chuckle at the disgusting taste of the okra.

When we finish eating, I place all the dishes in the sink. A white envelope rests on the sink's counter, quietly beckoning for attention. I hastily wipe my hands on my pants and seize the letter off the counter. Haleema's familiar handwriting adorns the front of the envelope, fueling my curiosity. With a swift motion, I tear open the top, eager to absorb her words. As I withdraw the paper, a small photograph slips from within, and lands face down on the floor, each inscribed with the name "Yusuf."

I retrieve one of the fallen pictures, turning it over to expose a tiny, cherubic face painted in hues of pink.

Yusuf. My son.

A surge of emotions wells up within me as tears gather in the corners of my eyes. I gaze at the captivating ebony eyes of the infant, snugly swathed in a sky-blue cloth, his full head of hair peeping out from beneath a snug cap.

I didn't make it back in time for our child's birth.

My trembling hands reach for the following photograph, unveiling Yusuf but a few weeks or months apart. His face blossomed, his once-rosy cheeks now fuller. Adorned in a onesie, he smiles as his fingers seem almost ethereal. I wish to hold my child close to my chest and feel his soft skin.

I soak in the images of my son as my heart fills with joy. My eyes shed tears as I try to rub my child's face in the pictures. Yusuf, you are so precious. You will live in my heart forever.

My attention returns to the pristine sheet of paper in my hands. I carefully read Haleema's words.

CHAPTER 12

HALEEMA'S LETTER

———

Janab,   *September 20, 1988*
*Loving someone is never easy. Our love is like a river of fire,
and I am drowning in the flames. My love grows stronger for
you with every passing second.*

*I miss you so much that my chest becomes tense when I
think about you. Sometimes at night, I think you are still next
to me. I reach out and tap your side of the bed, searching for
you, searching for your chest to rest my head on, searching
for your warmth when my blanket isn't enough, searching for
you when our son sheds tears. But you are not there. I hold
a pillow while sleeping, hoping never to forget how you feel,
hoping never to forget the feeling of our bodies intertwined.*

*I am starting to forget the rhythm of your heartbeat. One-
two, one-two, one-two. When I close my eyes, I can remember
how your hands feel against mine. Maybe in the same way you
can recognize the different feathers of the birds by recognizing
the softness.*

*I now understand how the moon must feel when it shines
so brightly at night. It's all alone in the sky, so bright you can't
see the sparkles in the sky. How the parakeets must feel locked
up in their cage with nowhere to go. Your mother only lets me*

leave the house every fifteen days to see my father. She says that since she is a daughter, she understands my pain of wanting to see my father. She tells me I must understand her feelings, like being away from you. She blames me for your departure. If anything is to happen to you, she will never forgive me.

People tease me daily, saying you will not return and that you found someone fairer than me to marry—that you have another wife in America keeping you occupied. I know that could never be true. Our love for each other is too strong.

Our son is getting bigger. He is starting to look a lot like you. The hair on Yusuf's head is thick, like a sea of rich blackness. He is trying to flip and crawl but gives up quickly.

Nothing like his father.

He is sweet and gentle.

Nothing like you.

He smiles when he sees his other baby cousins and has drawn a deep connection with his youngest chacha, Siraj. He must understand the meaning of blood being thicker than water. He smiles when the parrot talks to him and wants to hold the animal through the cage. He might be longing for his father the same way I am.

Now I understand how a lover must feel to be unloved.

Your father misses you more than you can imagine. He doesn't let any of us know. But no one is allowed to answer the door anymore but him. He wants to be the first person to hold you when you arrive. Only Allah knows when you will be able to return.

We used the money you sent to fix the leaking roof. When it rains, the water doesn't collect in buckets all night.

I know you are very far away, and no end is in sight. It must feel like you are back on the ship where all the eye can see is the ocean and no sign of life or land. I try not to think anything terrible will happen to you. I pray for your protection every day. Your name leaves my tongue every night. The fruit of patience is sweeter the longer one waits.

May Allah protect you every step of the way.

I pray for your protection.

Your wife,

Haleema

CHAPTER 13

TAXI

———

January 3, 1989

Floods of people pour out of the automatic airport doors, swirling like a chaotic torrent. The morning rush at the airport is like an unleashed pack of animals, always teeming with activity. Most of the passengers are clad in suits, complete with skinny ties, while the women sport tight skirts and high heels that echo on the concrete as they head to the waiting taxis.

Meanwhile, I patiently wait outside, my taxi stationed nearby, anticipating a customer. Another yellow envelope from home lay on the dashboard, beckoning me to read its contents during the lulls of incoming arrivals.

A tall white man with broad shoulders walks toward my taxi, wheeling a black suitcase. His eyes hold the marks of exhaustion, surrounded by dark circles, and the afternoon shadow from his earlier shave stretches across his face.

He gently taps the glass of the passenger window. "Can you take me to 20 John F. Kennedy Street?" he asks, his gaze scanning my seat, perhaps in search of a nametag or any indicator of my identity. "By the way, what's your name?

Usually, drivers have a name tag or something that displays their name."

"Jahangir," I blurt out without even thinking that I might want to give a fake name in case he files a complaint. I should have said Waheed's name; he's the one who can take the car.

"Take me near JFK. I'll know the building when I see it. I've been a million times," he says, making firm eye contact. The white part of his eyes is bright red and his hair only holds a few silver hairs.

The red-eyed man gets into the car and slams the door behind him loudly. He only carries one bag and places it on the seat beside him. He smells of strong scents of cologne with hints of orange blossom.

"What did you say your name was again?" he asks, looking straight into the rearview mirror, trying to keep firm eye contact even though my head is toward him and my eyes are on the road. Maybe this is an American thing like maintaining eye contact. To seem engaged. Or perhaps he's onto me. Maybe he can tell from my voice that I don't belong here or am a foreigner. Or worse, I am here without permission.

My palms get sweaty as I hold on to the rigged steering wheel. He's going to say something about my foreign name.

"Jahangir," I say, almost forgetting my name. I am sure he can hear my spurious English when I speak.

"Jahangir," he says, enunciating the a's in my name harshly and putting the wrong emphasis on the 'h' and 'g' in my name. "That's the name of that emperor. Isn't it?" His tone is curious.

I am caught off guard and not sure how to reply.

"That's who you're named after. Isn't it? He was a ruthless king during the Mughal reign. He killed his own sons or something like that and had twenty-six wives. I mean, can you imagine being married to so many princesses?" the white man says with a chuckle in his voice.

Ease falls upon me. The man was asking about my name, which was familiar to him.

"Jahangir was the emperor, and his son was Shah Jahan, the man who made the Red Fort and the Taj Mahal for his beloved wife, Mumtaz Mahal," I say.

"I know, Jahangir. I have been to the Red Fort and the Taj Mahal. I went to India not too long ago," the man says with an admirable confident voice.

"What were you doing in India?" I ask, surprised that a white man like him knows so much about my name.

"I was just there doing research with a few students. It was a completely different place. The clothes looked nothing like here, and the food was spicy. Are you from India?" the man asks while looking out the window.

"I'm from Pakistan. I came here a few months ago with a few animals, and well, I lost them, and now I drive around all day to see if I can find them," the words sound ridiculous as they leave my mouth.

"You are kidding or talking about your children?" the white man asks.

"I am just joking with you," I lie, not wanting to tell him the story and not knowing where to begin telling him about the ship, the zoo, Saife, or how I ended up here, driving him.

"When I was a student here, I drove a taxicab too," the man says.

"Really?" I respond in disbelief.

"I had no money, and my mom couldn't send me to college. So I got my lazy butt up and drove a cab until I graduated," he told me.

We continue driving in silence as the white man stares out the window. He doesn't ask me any other questions or say anything else until his destination arrives.

"Alright, Jahangir," he says my name again, emphasizing all the letters incorrectly. "This is where I get off. Can you tell me what the meter says?"

"Eleven dollars," I say as he hands me more cash than I request.

"Keep it," he says, slamming the door behind him and walking away.

His destination doesn't look like a house, apartment, or office building. He asked to be dropped off in the middle of Harvard Square, near the subway station. During the morning, the streets are crowded. Students with their Harvard sweaters and backpacks roam the streets.

He must be a professor at Tech of Harvard since he mentioned going to India for research.

It always surprises me when Americans know about Pakistan and more so if they have been anywhere near that area of the world. I don't usually get any customers in the taxi who even want to talk to me. They sometimes act like they can't understand what I am saying because of my accent. Regardless, this man was different and had a charm to him. For every American, I encounter a few hidden diamonds that make me feel like I do belong here and can live here among them.

This country will never feel like mine, and I will always feel like a servant to these white-skinned people. But some of them are different and see me as a part of the fabric of this country, not as a servant or a worker but as a person.

I stay parked in the spot and reach for the envelope. It's not as thick as the previous ones. I rip open the top, and white sheets of paper fall out.

CHAPTER 14

MAMA'S LETTER

———

Jahangir,   *November 27, 1988*
*Today is your birthday. My firstborn, tiny first son, and person
to teach me how to love something more than myself. I still
remember the sound of the call to prayer at the break of dawn
and your crying noise as I pushed you out.*
    *I cooked your favorite meal, stuffed okra and biryani. I'm
not sure if the others remember you were born on this day, but
a mother never forgets the nine months of pain.*
    *The smell of the spices and the tanginess on my tongue
reminded me of the way you like to lick the spices off the okra
before eating it.*
    *What are you eating in the United States of Amerika?
Haleema and I are not there to bring you warm rotis right
off the stove.*
    *Winter is about to begin. The floor will feel unusually colder
this time, the breeze will be chillier, and the moonlight brighter
in the clear skies. Everything will be more difficult without
you. Who will ensure their father wears the proper socks and
hat before entering the mosque? Your siblings are useless. I
wonder if they were brought up in the same womb as you. Or
what I must have eaten while they were still in my stomach for*

them to turn out this way. *They sit around all day bragging about their brother in Amerika to the neighborhood as if you are a celebrity.*

When your cousins from Peshawar visited, your siblings told these nonsensical stories about the zoo and how you would fight with tigers. The room would draw silent when I would walk in. Everyone but your cousins knows the lies. But your poor, gullible cousins would believe the tall tales too. They would believe the stories about you wrestling animals at the zoo and fighting people on the ship on your way to deliver the animals.

They also tell these ridiculous stories about you in Amerika, how you must be eating the best food, and how no one goes hungry in Amerika. You are dressing in the new clothes and brands they mention that I have never heard of.

Haleema has endured enough pain these past several months. She birthed a handsome baby boy, Yusuf, just like his father. She is waiting for your arrival every day, hoping one day you will be able to hold your flesh to your chest. We are all waiting for your return. A mother suffers silently, but I know Haleema needs her husband. It is not right for her to be spending months, almost a year, without you.

People taunt her saying her husband has forgotten about her in Amerika. It is as if she is waiting on the execution line, anticipating your bad fortune.

You don't understand how deeply a woman can love someone. How deeply a mother loves someone. You are a father now, but first, you are a provider and husband to your wife. You should not be a father if you cannot be a husband.

Your father's broad chest puffs out with pride at the sound of your name. He has never been more proud of anyone in his life. He feels you are a man who will carry on his legacy. Your *father left our village, our land, our homes, in Bhopal when Pakistan was created. A divide was created by the Muslims and Hindus. We left everything behind in search of a better life. We had nothing with us when we arrived in this home we now live in.*

Our homes, our land, and our memories remain. When we leave a place, a part of our soul gets left behind with the place. Millions of souls scattered on the land left, searching for a better life. He left his hometown with the three of you in his arms and on our shoulders. We had nothing but a few clothes wrapped in our bedsheets. We had nowhere to go, but your father was set on a mission to make it to the land made for Muslims.

You must have been too young to remember the first few years we moved. We ate nothing but plain rice. Your father roamed the streets looking for any place that would pay him a few rupees a week. I looked after you all and boiled rice to hand feed you. It was a strenuous time for us.

Until one day, your father stumbled upon a building being built. A lot of development was happening at the time we moved to make homes and space for those who arrived. They hired him to build. Every night he would come home sore, his muscles swollen, his hands cut up. He never enjoyed the fruit of his labor.

I am not sure why I am telling you all this now. You certainly do not have any memories of when your father worked all day and night to provide us with anything other than rice. Perhaps I imagine you are in the same situation, laboring away to give us a better life. Your soul is being squeezed out like water from a wet towel. You must be losing sleep just like your father was.

He is proud to call you his son. You left with nothing but the briefcase and the animals you needed to deliver and have made a life for yourself now. We are all proud of you. Now you must return and care for the wife and child you left behind.

May Allah protect you from the evil eye. I will pray for you and your health.

Your mother

CHAPTER 15

SCARLET

———

April 26, 1989

Silence engulfs the room as the rough texture of the sofa's fabric rubs against my face. Waheed and Saife return home, and the air becomes tainted with their sour scent. No one notices me resting while they enter the house. The parrot sleeps while perched in its cage. Soon, it would join the chorus of the waking world, singing and chirping with the sun. In the dimness of the room, I lack the motivation to illuminate it or prepare a meal. In just a few hours, I would have to venture back to the parking lot and embark on my taxi-driving duties, obliged to fulfill demands and field inquiries about my origin and journey. While staring at the parrot's downy feathers, my thoughts drift to the other creatures. Lost, like the shattered dreams and forsaken hopes of many men I now shared my life with.

How can a ship misplace containers housing something living? Imagine expecting a shipment of silk dresses or bananas, only to find a four-hundred-pound tiger lurking within. By now, someone should have discovered those animals. I hadn't arrived in this country to settle permanently, yet the passing days have morphed into weeks and the weeks into months. Over a year has passed since I last laid eyes upon my family.

The never-ending shifts at the parking lot have weighed heavily on me, leaving me perpetually on edge, fearing the repercussions of overstaying my welcome in this foreign land. Reclining on the sofa, I struggle to recall the sensations of home.

I long for the echoes of Haleema's laughter and the smooth touch of her skin. The way my fingers would intertwine with her lustrous hair as we embraced.

The strong stench of sweat enters the room as Waheed enters the dimly lit room.

"Jay, you awake?" Waheed asks.

"Yea, my next shift starts soon," I say hoarsely. "I was wondering if I should sleep or wait a little longer."

Saife shuffles into the living room, our voices waking him up and carrying him into the living room. "You guys don't even let me sleep on my one day off," he says, ferociously rubbing his eyes.

"Did you visit the port today?" Waheed asks.

"No, I didn't have time. I had to work." I want to evade the question. The animals haven't been on my mind for many weeks. I rise from the sofa and sit beside the table.

"Jay, you won't be able to stay here much longer. It doesn't matter what you think is right or wrong. If you want to stay in this country longer, I better see you at city hall tomorrow morning, ready to marry Scarlet from the garage. She's already agreed to sign the papers if you pay her the fee," Saife says.

I rest my forehead against the wobbly wooden table. Without even trying, the mere thought of the animals and the reasons that brought me to America tether me to this place, urging me to stay longer.

I meet his gaze, discerning the furrowed eyebrows that reveal his contemplation. "Jay, if you want to stay, you'll have to marry Scarlet," Saife says, his tone tinged with anxiety, awaiting my response.

But the truth is, I have no immediate reply. Staying here has become increasingly arduous. Earning enough elsewhere seems improbable, and returning home is not an option. I have tasted this foreign water and can never return to drinking any other kind.

"You just have to pay her to sign the marriage license. There's no other way for us to live here. After getting your green card, you file for divorce and return home. No one will ever even find out," Saife says while shaking his head and leaving the room in frustration with his arms in the air.

"I already spoke to her, and she'll meet you at ten o'clock at city hall. We can walk over together," Saife suggests.

But how can I? Me? How can I betray Haleema this way? I sink into my seat, my heart pounding in my chest. The feeling of dread gnaws away at my head.

No one can convince me. I will not marry someone so I can stay in this country. I have a wife—a wife, a love, and a child I haven't seen yet.

Lost in my thoughts, I get startled when Waheed speaks, "Naseem is going to do the same thing, Jay. I don't know why you are getting so emotional about it. We know you have a wife and kid—"

"Exactly, I have a wife and kid, and Naseem is alone," I blurt out. I gather my keys and abruptly walk away. I can't marry another woman just to stay in this country. Haleema will never forgive me. My father will never forgive me. I am not an unfaithful man.

I approach the bedroom door; my heart is heavy. Unable to contain my emotions any longer, I release a sigh. I smash my alarm clock on the ground, its shattered pieces mirroring the fragments of my broken soul.

Exhaustion courses through my veins and threatens to consume me entirely. The weight of the world seems insurmountable, draining my mind. I realize I cannot endure until my next shift, a few short hours away. But my mind and thoughts are all consumed by one person—Haleema.

As I rest on the mattress, it feels hollow, lacking the warmth and solace only Haleema's presence can provide. I close my eyes and imagine her delicate touch and how her embrace would engulf me, granting me refuge from the frigid emptiness. I yearn for Haleema's love to fill the void in my life, to wrap me in a blanket of affection.

The next morning, I stare at the dreary ceiling. I feel an indescribable urge to remain in bed with my eyes transfixed to the ceiling. Nothing is even there to capture my attention. Perhaps that or some unrecognizable force flings me out of bed and carries me to the bathroom.

Dried drool crusts at the corner of my mouth, and my eyelids bear the weight of dirt and oil. Exhausted, I glide the razor across my face, causing bright red spots to emerge on my swollen skin where blood trickles down. Seeking relief, I splash ice-cold water on my face, stirring a semblance of wakefulness. It's enough to regain my senses and present a cleaner appearance. I dab oil in my hair and return to the bedroom, where the resounding snores of fatigued, achy men fill the room. Their collective snoring resembles a struggling rickshaw trying to drive up a steep hill with the engine on the verge of surrender.

What are Waheed and Saife's plans for me today? They want me to get married to some stranger. I can't stoop so low as to forget about my wife and child and the commitment I granted them just to get married to stay here longer.

It's only a matter of a few hundred dollars, and I would be able to get my green card and see Haleema. I could hold my child to my chest and never let him go.

Marriage is the only way I can stay and bring Haleema here with me one day. No other options are left. No loopholes are left to get a green card. Saife and Waheed have tried everything to help me. We have lost so much money to lawyers asking to make fake claims saying we are here as asylum seekers.

I hope Haleema will understand and forgive me if she ever finds out. I will shield her from the marriage. It will be over before she even finds out. Nothing will get in the way.

I grab the shiny black shoes Haleema helped me polish the day I was leaving. Now I polish them alone to head over to do something that will hurt her more than is imaginable. She will never look at me the same.

I put on the only suit in the closet. Not sure who it belongs to, but it's one of the men living in this chaos of a home. I leave the room to find Waheed and Saife dressed and ready to go.

"Alhumdulliah. Thankful for Allah," Waheed says. "We were hoping you wouldn't change your mind. Jay, this is the only option left," he says, but I am still doubtful. I can still say no.

We arrive at city hall in Central Square across from the YMCA. The rustic cobblestone building has violet and red tulips planted on its lawn. An American flag hangs on the building, floating with the wind. We pass this massive building several times, unaware of its purpose.

My feet are glued to the sidewalk. I am unable to move up the stairs toward the front door. I have to carry myself up them. It feels as if my body is in molasses, struggling to move, as if I am dragging an anchor with every step I take.

The building smells of old wood, and I look around at the many windows and portraits of older men covering the walls. I can hear people clicking away on keyboards and the loud thumping sound of stamps hitting pieces of paper. Women yell at each other; others come with cash to settle debts or pay taxes.

"Scarlet said to meet her inside," Waheed says.

A feeling of dread overcomes me. There could have been another way.

Another wedding is taking place. I notice a woman elegantly attired in a pristine white gown, her hair gracefully concealed beneath a delicate laced veil. The bride with her head covered is somewhat familiar to me, as Haleema, too, covered her head at our wedding with vibrant red garments.

Amid the gathering, a young white woman arrives in a short white dress, revealing her knees. Her lips are covered in bright red lipstick, smudging on her chin, and her cheeks are a peach color.

"I'm Scarlet," she leans into me while whispering.

I am stiff as she embraces me. No one is going to believe she is getting married here.

A woman with short, ruby hair approaches us. "Alrighty now. Look at this beautiful couple." She points her hand at Scarlet and me. "My name is Nancy. I am the city clerk."

Scarlet is beaming, playing the role of bride better than she dressed up for it.

"Follow me into the chambers where we officiate weddings." The city clerk gestures for us to follow her, and we make our way up the wooden stairs, dodging other people coming down.

People congratulate Scarlet and me as we walk up a series of wooden stairs. We walk past another woman in an all-white dress with a white rose bouquet in her hands and pearl earrings.

Out of the corner of my eye, just as I'm getting wrapped in my thoughts, a woman approaches us.

"Hello and welcome! My name is Janice, and I will take you to the altar to get married. Follow me," she says quickly, walking up another set of wooden stairs lined with paintings of older men posing in black suits.

I still have time to walk out now. I need to leave, walk away, walk in the opposite direction. When my feet are just about to turn the other way—to leave, run away, and never come back—I feel Scarlet yank my arm. Her grip is such that I have no control over my body. I am like a puppet walking under the guise of my volition. But in reality, I wonder whether I can now squarely believe that fate is taking me up the stairs, led by this strange woman. We enter a room with wood all around it and portraits of people.

I see the altar, just like the ones in American movies, with an arch and a place for two people to stand across from each other. Janice ushers us to stand and places us in the right spots. Scarlet plays her part well and looks at me with tender eyes.

"Welcome, family and friends," Janice recites from a piece of paper. "We are gathered here today to witness and celebrate the marriage of Jahangir and Scarlet. This is not the beginning of a new relationship but an acknowledgment of the next chapter in their lives together. Today, they will affirm this bond formally and publicly. Jahangir and Scarlet will mark their transition as a couple by celebrating the love between themselves and the love between all of us. Today would be far less joyous without that love," she continues.

"Do you, Scarlet, take Jahangir to be your lawfully wedded husband?" Janice asks. "To have and to hold, in sickness and health, in good times and not so good times, for richer or poorer, keeping yourself unto him for as long as you both shall live?"

I close my eyes to pray. I ask my family for their forgiveness and my mother for her forgiveness.

"I do," Scarlet says without any hesitation.

I am holding Scarlet's sweaty hands, and I feel the weight of my hand slipping from her grip.

"Do you, Jahangir, take Scarlet to be your lawfully wedded wife?" Nancy asks as the sweat collects on my forehead. My stomach turns, and I feel nauseated. I want to throw up, to let out all my thoughts and frustrations.

"To have and to hold, in sickness and in health, in good times and not so good times, for richer or poorer, keeping yourself unto her for as long as you both shall live?" Janice stops, looks over at me, and raises her eyebrows. She has a concerned look on her face.

Scarlet forces a smile on her face and rubs my hand.

I can still say no. I can turn back. I can leave this room, walk down those city hall steps and never return to this place. My wife and child are waiting for me back home. They will never forgive me when they learn about this. Me, marrying another woman I don't even know. I don't love her. She means nothing to me.

Wiping the sweat off my head, I hear my name again.

"Jahangir?" Janice says, emphasizing the wrong letters in my name. She says it so incorrectly it sounds foreign to my ears.

There's no turning back for me.

After a long pause, I finally let out the words from my mouth. "I do," I turn to look Scarlet in the eyes; she beams with joy. Although we are strangers, one would never think this is the first time we met from the sparkle in Scarlet's eyes.

I loathe her happiness. How effortless it is for her to look in love. How easy. How cruel it feels to me. Dread hangs over me like a dark cloud.

"Now is time for the ring exchange," Janice says. I pat my pants and realize I do not have a ring for Scarlet. In our traditions, we usually do not exchange rings. We sign a few papers after being asked if we want to marry the person in front of us and that is it; we are married under the eyes of Allah.

Waheed and Saife pat me on the shoulder and hand me a ring. "She will give it back after this," Waheed whispers in my ear.

"A ring is an unbroken circle, with ends that have been joined together, and it represents your union. It is a symbol of infinity and of your infinite love. When you look at these rings on your hands, be reminded of this moment, your commitment, and the love you now feel for each other." Janice pauses.

"Scarlet, place the ring on Jahangir's finger and repeat after me. Jahangir, I give you this ring as a symbol of my love with the pledge: to love you today, tomorrow, always, and forever," Janice says slowly.

"Jahangir, I give you this ring as a symbol of my love with the pledge to love you today, tomorrow, always, and forever," Scarlet recites as she slides the ring onto my finger.

The cold metal around my finger reminds me of the steel from the ship.

"Jahangir, place the ring on Scarlet's finger and repeat after me. Scarlet, I give you this ring as a symbol of my love with the pledge to love you today, tomorrow, always, and forever."

I look at Scarlet and say, "I give you this ring as a symbol of my love with the pledge to love you today, tomorrow, always, and forever." I look away and mutter to myself, "Haleema, my love."

My heart twists in a knot, and the guilt overflows within. Haleema will understand what I had to do to stay here longer. Our love for each other is forgiving. I stretched the limits of our love. I will never let her find out about my actions. The shame and guilt will eat me alive for the rest of my life, pushing me to be an even better husband and father.

"Before these witnesses, you have pledged to join in marriage. You have now sealed this pledge with your wedding rings. By the power vested in me by the great state of Massachusetts, I now pronounce you husband and wife. You may now kiss the bride." Janice closes her folder as Scarlet, and I exchange a small peck on the lips.

Her lips are thin, crackly, and harsh—nothing like the soft pillows of Haleema's lips.

I glance at Waheed and Saife, who give me two thumbs up each. It all looks so unreal to be marrying Scarlet.

"We need our witnesses," Janice says, looking over at Waheed and Saife. "Please, hurry up." She rushes them. Maybe she senses a fraud in our wedding.

"Congratulations. You are now husband and wife," Janice says while her eyes fixate on me. I hear a sharpness to her voice, almost like a threat. As I grab the papers, she holds on a bit longer. She must know that I am only getting married for these papers. She releases the paper, jerking my hand back a little bit.

Scarlet holds my hand and leans into me, trying to kiss me again. I move my face away from hers. Opening the folder, I can now prove that I am married to a woman here and can apply for my green card. Soon enough, I will end this marriage with Scarlet and bring my wife here. Haleema will never find out about this. If she finds out, she will be crushed forever. I don't think she could ever forgive me for such an act.

Scarlet and I walk out of city hall together. My legs feel lighter walking down the stairs. The weight of my decision no longer pushes me down.

"We don't need to pretend that much, big guy," she says while letting go of my hand.

"You don't need to live with me until the papers come. They probably won't come looking for you or looking to see if we are married. But I will add you to my insurance and put some men's shoes by the front door, a razor in the bathroom, and I have my ex's clothes in the closet anyway," she says. This isn't her first time doing something like this.

"It will look like we are married. We can use the insurance as proof, but don't get hurt or anything. Do you understand?" she asks.

I'm not following all of her words. I am in a state of shock yet relieved that I can live here a bit more peacefully. I won't have to worry every time I hear the sirens of cop cars and think they will come after me.

"Thank you, Scarlet," I say, looking into her shimmery blue eyes.

"Oh, and last thing before you run off," she says, tugging my arm. "I'll file for the divorce a few months after you get your green card in the mail. Normally, that's enough time to pass off the marriage. I doubt anything will happen after that." She hands me the marriage certificate.

I walk away with the marriage license. All I need to do is get a few more pieces of evidence from Scarlet, and I can apply for a green card. For months now, I worried about finding my animals when the animals were unattainable; I worked to provide for my family endeavors, fearing I wouldn't be able to stay for long without papers. And now, I have the papers, but it still doesn't give me the relief I hoped for. This shouldn't have been the way to go about it.

CHAPTER 16

HALEEMA'S LETTER

———

Meri Jaan,   *June 19, 1989*
*Today, I visited Sea View with Bhaijaan, his wife, and the
children. We cramped inside the car, sitting one on top of the
other. It was nothing like my empty bed without you. My body
stays in one place, afraid to feel the cold sheets inches away
from me in every direction.*

   *As we arrived, the smell of the salty ocean pulled us closer.
The salt in the breeze and the crashing waves made me nostalgic
for you. I remember we would walk along the sea, letting our feet
sink into the sand and leaving behind our footsteps. My mind
and thoughts would drift away with the sounds of the water hitting against my legs and causing the cotton of my pants to stick
to my skin. You'd look at me with sparks in your eyes, and I'd
look away with flushed cheeks—not knowing one day that those
footsteps would drift away in the ocean, far from me.*

   *Sea View was like heaven with you, but now it feels like a
desert of sorrow. I want to write your name on every grain of
sand and every droplet of water to show you how lonely I am.
My tears flow out of my eyes like the ocean.*

   *Bhaijaan and I drank chai at one of the stalls. The screech-
ing sound of the plastic chairs being pushed together reminded*

me how you'd push your chair next to mine while we shared a snack. Now, our child tries to hold on to them while attempting to lift himself up to walk. He cries terribly whenever the camels walk by. I think he's scared of them. Terrified.

Everything reminds me of you these days. It's been over a year since we said goodbye at the port. We released each other's hands as the port rocked with every crashing wave. I wasn't sure when I would hear from you or what the journey would look like. But I couldn't imagine these days feeling like months in your absence.

The NADRA office is of no help, and neither is the embassy. I went to the office and asked how I could get a visa to visit you. They laugh in my face. Papa tells me to bring our son with me. Yusuf's bold eyes and flirty lashes will help me plead my case for a visa to see you.

Every day I show Yusuf pictures of his handsome father. I point to the picture we took of you at the port, trying to teach him that this is Papa. He mutters his own words while holding your photo. We all laugh in excitement that he is learning and recognizing people around him.

I started teaching again. The students arrive at the house right before maghrib and leave when they complete their tasks. You must know all the children. They come from the flat you were raised in. Children of the neighbors you grew up with. Some of the students bring their younger siblings along with them, and I bribe them with little sweets and try to teach them the alphabet. A for apple, B for Boy, and C for Cat. At cat, I meow to make them giggle.

Sometimes our son crawls to join the students. He loves the attention he gets from all of them. They will pass him along like a toy doll as they sit in a circle and complete their home-work or additional assignments I create for them. They also use his cuteness against me, playing with him to avoid doing their homework. *Their parents have permitted me to spank them if they don't listen, but I would never lay my hands on those innocent children. They don't understand what's right from wrong. They learn from examples. If I start hitting them whenever they mess up on their homework, they will think that is the right way to communicate.*

Yesterday, when I went to the market, the vegetable vendor said my face looked pale, and I was losing the color in my face in anticipation of my husband. When I walked by the roses in the market, it reminded me of our wedding night. Hundreds of thousands of petals covered the bed when you brought me inside. My skin smelled of roses for days, and our room smelled like the market for weeks. The smell is so strong in my head that whenever I smell a rose, I think of your soft skin against mine.

Jahangir, my heart calls for you. My soul weeps for you. My body longs for you. When are you returning? We have a life here. We have our family here. We have everyone we know here. I am beginning to think I should stop using we and instead refer to our marriage as you and me. You have added so much distance between us.

It feels like a morgue at home without you. I feel like a lifeless corpse going about my daily tasks. You are to me what water is for our Earth. Survival. I can't live without you.

Please write back or send a signal that you are doing well. We pray for you in every prayer. Five times a day, I ask for my husband back. I never miss a chance to say your name while I am on my knees making dua.

My love for you aches. I love you more than anyone.
Your wife,
Haleema

CHAPTER 17

QUARTERS

———

January 17, 1990

The same grain-skinned man walks in again, setting off the bell at the door. He drops a ten-dollar bill and asks for a roll of quarters. He never shops around the store—no lottery tickets. No liquor. Just quarters. He comes to the store at least once or twice a week.

His hands are vast and rugged with black stains under his nails. His skin is just like mine. He doesn't look too different from my people, but I know he isn't from my homeland.

He pulls out a crisp ten-dollar bill from his pocket and places it on the table. It's a routine for us now. He doesn't even say a word. He seems distracted and distressed. His hair is flat, as if he has worn a hat all day.

"My friend, what do you do with these quarters?" I finally find the courage to interact with him and ask him.

"I use the phone. Talk to my family," he says, avoiding eye contact.

"Where is your family?" I ask while getting the register keys.

"Guadalajara," he says. The letters leave his mouth in an accent foreign to my ears.

Guadalajara. It's not a place I have ever heard of. Perhaps, it's a city here in Massachusetts.

"Where is that?" I ask.

"It's in Mexico," he responds.

I hear the accent in his voice as the words leave his mouth. Mexico. I look at his hands again. He is in some sort of manual labor job, either as a farmer or construction worker, causing his hands to shift to adjust to the rough conditions he works in.

I hand him back the ten-dollar bill. I am not taking out the rolls of quarters for him.

"Are you going to talk to them right now?" I ask.

His forehead creases. He doesn't seem to understand. I point at my phone under the counter and ask, "Do you want to talk to them now?"

"That won't dial," he responds. There are several area codes and numbers to dial before being able to call.

"I can do it. Give me the number of your family." I print out a white receipt and hand him a pen. "Write down the number."

He scribbles a series of numbers on the paper, his hand moving almost desperately. He thrusts the paper toward me.

Grasping the phone tightly, I dial the numbers Waheed told me to dial when I want to speak to my family. It's not a legal way of reaching my family, but it is a cheap alternative. Conscious of the need for secrecy, I motion for the man to avert his gaze.

The sound of the ringing fills the space around us. I feel sweat collecting on my forehead, hoping the other end will be his family and not something else. The phone continues to ring.

On the third ring, a crackling sound disrupts the ringing, accompanied by a muffled sound uttered by a lady on the line. Her words float in the air, elusive and incomprehensible. "Here, it's for you," I say, breaking the silence and handing over the phone to the man. His eyes widen with disbelief. "Take it. Say something," I urge, extending the device toward him. His fingers close around the sleek black body of the phone, raising it slowly to his ear.

"Hallo," he utters tentatively. A burst of laughter escapes his lips, followed by a stream of unfamiliar words that dance in the air, captivating and foreign.

"Talk for as long as you want. There's no charge," I assure him, aware that my shift will soon end and Waheed will arrive quickly.

The door's chime echoes as the man immerses himself in the conversation. Waheed strides in, his arms laden with a towering stack of books. In the solitude of the night shift, where customers are scarce, he seizes this opportunity to catch up on his studies. The silence of the night grants him uninterrupted hours to study for his exams, a luxury he can't afford during the day.

As I watch him pour over his textbooks, I can't help but wonder if it's worth it for him. I see the stress on his face, from his droopy eyes and his shoulders rising from having to work so hard to send money back to his family. His parents and siblings all rely on him.

Waheed shuffles through his stack of books on the counter and hands me the keys. "You can take the taxi now, Jay. Did Scarlet say anything about when your card will arrive in the mail?" Waheed asks.

"No," I solemnly say. I long for that card in the mail that would end things with me and Scarlet. I'd be on the first flight back to Haleema.

"It's only been a few weeks," Waheed says, flashing his charming smile. "I'm sure it will be here in no time."

While he works at the gas station, I take my shift in the taxi—from four in the morning 'til four in the afternoon. If it's slow, I head home, not wanting to waste my time driving around the city.

"Oh shit," I hear Waheed say. "I forgot my chemistry book, and I have an exam tomorrow morning in that class. Jay, can you bring my book when you head out to drive the taxi? It has a purple cover and says chemistry on it in big purple letters. Can you do that?"

"You need it now?" I ask, making sure.

"You can bring it in a few hours; I have these worksheets to do," he holds up stacks of paper while pleading.

"I'll get it. And Waheed, he's talking to his family. Don't bother him," I let Waheed know, pointing at the man on the phone.

"What would I do? I don't care if he's on the phone. You think I am a police officer." He laughs.

Grabbing the keys from him, I drive back to the apartment.

The drive back is silent, the only sound coming from the car's engine. Darkness shrouds the streets. Even birds are quiet, leaving only the hum of my car engine to break the eerie quiet.

I get back to the apartment at nearly sunrise. I only have a few more hours to head out to the airport. The apartment is far from silent like the streets; the loud snoring sounds of exhausted men echo throughout the apartment.

Walking into the living room, I see sleeping bodies occupying every inch of the room. I sit on the cold floor and lean against the wall, waiting for someone else to wake up and make it to their next shift for me to lie down for a few hours. There's only so much space for all of us. But like Saife said, you need space in your heart, not the room to make everyone fit.

I feel someone nudge me. I must have fallen asleep while leaning against the wall.

"Jao—go," I hear a voice in the dark say to me. The silhouette of his body and a finger point at an empty spot in the masses of bodies.

I lie down on the mattress, still warmth from whoever slept before me.

My eyes feel like they only blink, and it's time to wake up again. Still dark outside. Still unable to make out everything in the room.

My stomach growls. The sound reminds me of how the tigers roared in their cages when they smelled the meat during feeding time, but there is no food here. We aren't able to eat more than one meal a day anyway.

After failing to find anything in the cabinets, I stumble to the taxi. I scan for Waheed's textbooks. I can't remember which one he said to bring, the purple one or the blue one, so I take both of them and head back to the gas station.

I walk into the convenience store, and the bell on the door rings as I enter.

"Jay!" I hear Waheed say in excitement.

"Here is your book." I hand over the book and notice fruit crates behind the counter. Is the store going to start selling fruits?

"Jay, that man you gave the phone to, he dropped off all this fruit for us," Waheed says. "His father passed away recently, and he's been trying to speak to family daily. He can't leave the country. Otherwise, he won't be able to get back. He was thrilled that you dialed the phone for him."

"Eat some! The taste of these is almost as sweet as the fruit back home." Waheed grabs some grapes and hands them to me.

I pick up a cluster of grapes. They crunch as I bite into them, releasing a burst of sweet juices. These grapes are straight from the farm, radiating freshness. With each bite, I savor their flavor, reminiscent of the sweet taste of fruits from my homeland. Memories flood my mind of Mama cutting a bowl of assorted fruits for us after dinner every night. I didn't fully appreciate those moments back then, but now I long for them, realizing how much I took them for granted.

Signs of stress covered the face of the man with the quarters. The dirt on his hands reveals that he works on a farm, but I never anticipated his gesture of gratitude—a bountiful offering of fruits—as a repayment for a simple phone call. I helped the man because so many have helped me. Despite this country's hardships, it continues to bless us with its generosity.

As I reach over to grab more fruit for the road, the sudden sound of loud, piercing noises fills the room. Without hesitation, Waheed yanks both of my hands, pulling me under the counter. My shoulder stretches out painfully. My eyes shut, and a blinding blackness and a loud, piercing sound flood my head. I think my skull is about to explode.

CHAPTER 18

SHOT

———

January 18, 1990

A sharp pain pierces my head as I slowly open my eyes. Then it shifts to my shoulders before emanating down my spine to my thighs and feet as I wiggle around the bed. A warm liquid drips along the left side of my face.

A dark cloud rolls through my head like a storm moving across the fields. I am unsure where I am. A dusky haze is in front of me.

I move my ponderous head around and see that I am home. How did I get home last night? Who put me to bed? I look down at my clothes, and I am still wearing my uniform and name tag with "Jay" written in metal still pinned to me.

I feel a stinging sensation on my hands from red scratch marks covering my hands and arm. I can't remember what happened, and the pain in my head won't let me complete a thought.

Strange chills run down my back as I try to get up. I look at the clock and see it is almost time to get to my shift at the convenience store. I just returned from the parking lot to my next shift.

I am glued to the bed, unable to move. Before I can push myself out of bed, Saife forcefully kicks the door open. He is panting as worry fills his eyes.

"Ya, Allah," Saife holds my head in his hands. "We thought we were going to lose you. What were you thinking trying to be a hero at the store? What if you lost your life?" Saife goes on about what I was doing.

I can't remember anything he is talking about. I feel warm water dripping from my head. I touch it and look at the liquid; dark red sticky blood coats my fingers.

"Waheed brought you here. He's coming back. I think you almost got shot in the head," he says in between sobs. "But it missed you. I can't take you to the doctor 'cause we don't want trouble," he frantically says.

Shot? I can't remember anything.

"What if you get caught? We can't take you there. Waheed is coming," Saife says frantically.

I must have blacked out from fear. I touch the warm liquid dripping down my face. It feels like a thicker sweat. I wipe the droplets, irritating my face and tickling me as they approach my cheek. The pain is worse than when I was attacked by the tiger and worse than leaving my family.

I can see my family standing in the room with me. I blink, and they are gone. I open my eyes again and sit in my living room with Papa. I am laughing and sitting near his feet below him.

A few more moments, please.

Haleema is there too. Her knees are drawn up close to her chest—the dark kohl on her inner lash line smudging toward the end of her misty eyes. I smile, looking at her and wanting to hold her close to me.

A few more minutes, please.

I hear sounds approaching, running up the stairs in a hurry with something jiggling in his hands. Waheed comes running inside.

No, please. I am with my family—one more minute with them. I barely spent time with them.

Just one more moment together.

"Jay, everything is going to be fine. Look at me." Someone shakes my face. My eyes roll back in my head. I drift away in search of home.

His warm hands rest on top of my head. Soft cotton balls push into the side of my head, tapping hard to get all the blood. I hear him speaking but can't make out any of the words. I feel I'm drifting in and out of reality. The world in front of me becomes blurry, shifting side by side.

"Do you see the bullet?"

"Is he going to be okay?"

"How did this even happen?"

Several different voices and different people come closer to me.

I shut my eyes.

Feeling a burning sensation, I jolt awake and fling myself up from the bed, my eyes widening in terror. I want to scream, but my voice fails me.

"It's fine, Jay. Just lie down." Waheed's voice breaks through the pain as he pushes my shoulder down on the bed.

"The bullet grazed you. There is a lot of blood, but you will be fine. I am stitching you up now, and the blood will stop," he continues, but his words trail off.

I am devoid of any emotions or strength to move or cry.

Waheed pauses for a second, and I hear him shouting at Saife to grab something. I can't figure out what he is saying.

The next thing I feel are tiny repeated stings going into my head like a swarm of bees attacking me.

I close my eyes and hope never to open them again.

When I open my eyes, the stinging and pain has lessened. Waheed and Saife's heads rest beside the mattress. Saife is still holding on to my clammy hand. I can feel the blisters on the palm of his hand. Toward my other hand, two envelopes lie next to me. It must be another letter from my family.

I look around to see the time but cannot move my head. The pain shoots throughout my body. I look around and see it's the middle of the day, around 1:00 p.m.

"Waheed," I say loudly enough to barely even reach my ears. "Waheed... Saife..." I speak a bit louder.

I pick my hand up and drop the weight into Saife's hand. Saife and Waheed both jolt off the mattress.

"Jay, you're awake. How are you feeling?" Waheed asks while reaching for my head.

"I got some medicine. The stitches will heal on their own, and lucky for you, the scar won't be bad. The bullet grazed you with no damage other than a bucket of blood. We are taking care of that." As Waheed speaks, Saife slowly wakes up too.

"You can't even think about going to work for the rest of the week. You need to rest," Saife says.

"Saife is right, Jay. You can't go back to work. Saife and I already went through your wallet and found who you've been sending money to in Pakistan and sent it for this month," Waheed says.

"Why did you do that?" I manage to say.

"Because we are a family," Waheed says while checking on the stitches in my head. He leaves the room and walks toward the kitchen. Saife joins him and brings back a bowl of warm soup. I don't know how to thank them. I am so grateful for these new brothers.

"I'm only doing this because you saved my life, Jay." Waheed laughs as Saife places the warm bowl on the table.

Slowly, I recall what happened the night before. I remember hearing the loud explosion, sounding like fireworks in my skull.

Waheed yanked my hands and dragged me over the counter. These men with masks and guns came running toward the register, kicking it at us and telling us to open it and give them all the money. Another man with a mask was at the door holding it open.

One of them slammed the bottom part of his gun into Waheed's head. So I shoved the man against the counter. We wrestled back and forth on the floor. My shoulders, arms, and face were scratched up. I was yanking on the back of his head and punching his face. The man at the door saw us wrestling back and forth and shot at me, missing enough for me to live.

The men ran away, and Waheed quickly rushed me home in the taxi, locking the store behind him.

"Make sure you eat enough." Saife pats my head endearingly. "You are going to be fine."

"There's another letter for you. Your father's words will give you strength, and the next envelope will give you a reason to live again," Waheed says as he leaves the room.

Papa's words have always provided me with strength.

I tear open the envelope; I hold a card with my name and picture printed. Tears pour down my face. It's my green card—finally here. I can see my family again. The tears flow like a river down my face as snot drips from my nose. I gasp for air in between my tears.

I am given another chance at life and another chance to see my family. All that needs to happen is for Scarlet and me to separate, and I can return home. I'll bring everyone back to Cambridge with me.

I tear open the other envelope. Unfolding the pieces of paper, I make out the letters. It's Papa's handwriting. I hold the pieces of paper in my hand. The pages smell like home—a mixture of cloves, fennel seeds, and affection.

His prayers have been answered. I will be able to return home.

I unfold the papers and read.

CHAPTER 19

PAPA'S LETTER

————

Raja,   *November 3, 1989*
You are spoiling us with the amount you send us. Every month when I collect the amount, I lie to your siblings about how much we have received so they do not become used to it. You do not need to support them for the rest of your life. I always remind them that it's temporary and that they should not get used to it. They should not use this money to get married and start families. It's one thing to pay for your sisters and another to support your brothers.

They are men just like you. They can take a leap of faith to start a business or a restaurant. A man needs to provide for his family. I wish I could do more for you—how you are doing for the rest of us now.

After Jummah this afternoon, I went to greet the imam. As we exchanged embraces, I could smell the strong scent of ittar on him, smelling like the earth and a hint of sweetness through roses. He mentioned that I am fortunate to have a son like you—to have made it away from here and created a better life for himself and those around him.

Even in the market, I walk with my head held high. The vendors will ask about my son and how he's made it outside of here and now providing for his family. They pray for a son like mine. While I pray for my son's return. No amount of money can replace your presence here. And now you have decided to live there. When do you plan to return?

I long for the days when you'd return from the zoo, sometimes carrying a feather or two with you, and would join me for prayer every dhuhr.

It's hard to believe it has been over a year since you left. We are still anticipating your return. We need to exchange so many words with one another, so many conversations left to have together.

I still need to teach you how to build a wooden chair. I have been building chairs all my life and hoping I would pass down this skill to you. If you have nothing else, at least you can make a handmade chair. I know the Westerners loved my handmade wooden things from our shop. It still saddens me to think about how modern technology ruined our little shop. I used to spend hours every day making little things for tourists who would travel to Pakistan.

Now the tourists are gone because of the ongoing wars. There are no wars here, but they think we are all the same. And the wood is gone because the factories and machines can make them faster and cheaper. Everything is being replaced with more rapid and more affordable technology. We will live in a world of machines and have no use for people.

But hopefully, we will still find use for our trade in a family. And we will still find use in each other.

I know you have found a way to make calls here. I heard your voice for the first time in many months. My heart raced. It felt as if you had returned, as if I could have embraced you to my chest. We all wait by the phone every time it rings. We hope it is your voice on the other side. Haleema sometimes walks around the area where the phone is, trying to be the first one to answer anytime it rings. She is always heartbroken when it is anyone else, even when someone from her family calls to check on her.

Raja, we are waiting for your return. I pray for you five times a day and hope you will return the way we sent you off. I would have never let you on the ship if I knew you would not return. Take care of yourself and remember to eat enough. Your mother is not there to make you daal and warm rotis with every meal. I am not there to add more to your empty plate. May Allah protect you from nazar, and may you remember us in your prayers. Please return home to us.

Allah Hafiz,
Your Papa

CHAPTER 20

GREEN STREET

——

June 14, 1990

As I stand in the concrete box of Green Street Garage with my coworker Abel, the air is heavy with the scent of exhausted fumes and motor oil, mingling with the occasional whiff of fast-food grease drifting in from the nearby McDonald's. The dull hum of car engines and the screech of tires fill the air.

Abel, a tall and slender man with dark glistening skin, stands beside me, accompanied by his youngest daughter. Her presence adds a touch of innocence and vibrancy to our surroundings. I catch a glimpse of Abel's pearly smile, radiant against the dimly lit garage. The fluorescent lights cast a yellow glow on his face.

Sliding the glass window open, I reach out to collect the parking tickets and cash from customers. Their screeching tires echo as they approach the exit booth. Often, they barely spare me a glance, treating my presence as that of a mere servant. Some customers dismissively toss their tickets and cash my way with their eyes fixed on the exit, awaiting my permission to pass.

As my shift nears an end, I run through my closing tasks. The cool touch of the metal register against my fingertips brings me back to the ship. I count the cash, feeling the texture of each soft bill as I stack them by numbers. The faint sound of rustling money fills my ears as I jot down the total amount and the date on the clipboard. I place the used parking tickets in a plastic box and hand them to Abel.

"You can put the rest of the tickets in here," I inform him, my voice carrying a hint of bittersweet anticipation. "And Abel, today is my last day. I'm going to see my family back in Pakistan." My words are cheerful.

"That's wonderful," he responds, his arms enfolding me in an embrace as he pats my back.

"How long will you be gone?" Abel asks, his daughter starting to whine in the background. He scoops her up in his large arms, and the weight of her petite body rests against his chest. He rubs her back in a soothing rhythm, attempting to hush her cries. At that moment, I yearn for the day when I can embrace my child, providing a source of comfort.

"I'm not sure, but maybe a couple of months. I want to bring my wife back with me now that all the other marriage stuff is over," I respond, my discomfort momentarily overshadowed by thoughts of Scarlet.

"I am so happy for you," Abel says, his sparkling teeth visible as he smiles. "I want to go back to Ethiopia and see my mother." He shares his desires.

"God willing, you will return," I reply, my hand reaching out to pat his shoulder one last time.

Leaving behind the concrete confines of Green Street Garage, I step out onto the bustling streets. I hurry down Green Street onto Mass Ave and cut through the yard to return home. Students juggle balls and feed the squirrels. I hurry along the familiar path, feeling the softness of the grass under my shoes. I rush home to say goodbye to Saife and Waheed before they leave for their shifts. I stumble through the front door and open the gold handle to our apartment. To my surprise, I find Saife and Waheed waiting for me. Their soft smiles light up the room. "Jay, I am really going to miss you," Saife says as he tightly embraces me. His head rests against my chest, and his chest rises and falls with his breath. I feel his silent prayers reverberate through his body, a wish for my safe return.

"I will be back," I reassure him.

"But who knows how long that could take," Waheed interjects. "And you won't be living with us when you bring your wife and child," he continues.

"I will always be near," I inform them. "And I will leave the gray parrot here as a reminder," I say, pointing at the parrot perched in its cage. Its feathers catch the light peering through the window.

Saife and Waheed are brothers to me. The ache of leaving them behind reminds me of my departure from my family in Karachi. As I long to return home, the emotions swirl within, a blend of pain and anticipation. If only I could bring these new brothers with me.

"Go get your things, and we'll drop you off at the airport," Waheed says, breaking the silence. My heart hurts from the impending farewell.

I rush into the living room and grab the smooth handle of my packed suitcase. Its weight reminds me of my heavy decision. With a final glance at the scattered room and broken furniture, I leave the apartment.

As I roll the suitcase down the hallway, the wheels get caught on the maroon carpet. I reach Waheed's taxi, its metal body glistening under the orange hues of the setting sun.

The warm rays cast a golden glow on the buildings and trees around us.

Sitting in the taxi's front seat beside Waheed, I hear the faint murmur of the radio seeping into the cab. The glimpses of city hall evoke a mix of nostalgia and anticipation. I know I will be back with my family once again.

Upon reaching the airport, the taxi comes to a halt, and Waheed steps out to get my bag. As he places the bag on the curb, he jokes, "That will be fifteen dollars, and I want a tip."

We share one last embrace. I feel the warmth of Saife's body seeping into mine. I also feel the dampness of sweat collecting on his back. Saife rubs his eyes to hold back tears that threaten to spill over.

I walk through the double doors and wave goodbye one last time. I see Waheed's arm wrapped around Saife's shoulders. Saife's cheeks glisten as Waheed comforts him.

I turn away and realize I am once again leaving loved ones. But as I feel the pain of departing, the thought of reuniting with Haleema and the rest of my family back home propels me forward. I left home for a task and a chance to do something better. Now my instincts return me home, reminding me nothing is better.

CHAPTER 21

RETURN

———

June 16, 1990

A hot gust of wind almost pushes me off the stairs leading off the plane. The aroma of home is in the air as if the street vendors are just a few inches away with their fried foods for me to devour. I am only a few steps out of my flight and have entered a new world.

After clearing immigration, I enter a crowd of hundreds of people. Some men hold up signs with names written in Urdu, and large families wait for their loved ones to arrive. In front of me, I watch a family embrace a man, covering him with kisses, tears, and sweat. I take a few more steps toward the crowd, scanning the faces to see any familiar ones.

"Raja bhai!" I hear someone shout. I look to my left and recognize my brother's face among the bustling crowd. He sprints toward me, his arms outstretched, and engulfs me in a tight embrace, lifting me off the ground. I spot my other relatives, cousins, and their children.

Between the whirlwind of emotions, I am passed from one family member to another, like a ball in a game of catch. The air fills with joyous laughter and affectionate kisses from my adoring aunts. My cousins take charge of my suitcases, allowing me to fully immerse myself in warm embraces with my aunts and uncles.

My eyes lock on to familiar faces through the bustling crowd—Papa and Haleema. Cradled in Haleema's arms, a child, his head nestled against her shoulder. My son. A heavy weight settles in my chest. Time seems to have only enhanced Haleema's beauty since our parting nearly two years ago. Her eyes are lined with the same allure of black kohl, and her silky hair peeps out from beneath her delicate chiffon scarf.

Papa approaches at a measured pace, aided by a cane and a noticeable limp. His free hand tightly clasps Haleema's arm, a steady anchor in their embrace.

"Raja," he whispers, cradling my face in his weathered hands. Tears stream down his weathered face. "It has been an eternity," Papa murmurs, drawing me closer to his chest and enfolding me in his arms.

Tears cascade down our cheeks. Memories flood my mind—the scent of his letters pressed against his chest, the fragrance that clung to his skin. His racing heart matches the rhythm of his large, gentle hands caressing the back of my head.

Haleema rests her hand on my back, and I hear her say in a soft, hush tone, "Bus—*enough*. Papa, you will get sick if you keep crying." She is rocking our son back and forth on her hip.

"Look at my son." I take the child from her and hold him close to my heart. "He's even more handsome than I thought," I say, lifting him high to get a good look at him. He looks almost exactly like Haleema. He has the same large dark eyes, plump lips, and hardly any traces of me. I pepper his face with kisses. His delicate features scrunch up, and he wails. He doesn't know who I am. To him, I am merely a stranger.

"Chalo, let's go," Papa pats my back and ushers us toward the car. "Raja, your mother is waiting for you at home. She wanted to meet you in the comfort of our own house."

I return our crying son to Haleema's arms.

Glancing back, I see the smiling faces of my cousins, aunts, and uncles. Around thirty people must have been eagerly waiting for me at the airport. My cousins load their cars while I settle in the seat next to Papa and Haleema as we drive home.

On the drive, I admire the Urdu words painted on walls and billboards. No trees line the roads nor any tall buildings with glossy exteriors. Instead, carts of food vendors stretch across every corner along the streets. As we come to a stop, people rush to our car, attempting to sell us jasmine flower bracelets and squeaky cartoon balloons. Yusuf eagerly reaches for the balloons, but Haleema grabs his hand. Another vendor approaches our window, offering salty popcorn bags.

The streets are bustling even at this late hour. Back in Cambridge, when I drove a taxi during this time, the silence unsettled me. I never knew who I could turn to if something terrible happened.

As we arrive home, family members gather outside the door to greet me.

The home looks different and newer. The glass on the windows is no longer shattered. The brown stains on the roof are plastered over. Even the fan, spinning in a circle, no longer makes a ticking sound. I take a few steps inside and realize the floor tiles are porcelain white, and a stove is inside without a gas tank next to it.

There are lights in the living room in preparation for my sister, Goodi's wedding. The festivities will begin tomorrow night.

Mama makes her way toward me. She has teary eyes as she wraps her hands around my neck. Her head falls right under my chin. I can smell the olive oil still in her hair. I see more grays now too.

"Come, let's go inside and eat," Mama says as she pulls my hand to the dining area. A new china cabinet sits against the wall, displaying glass dishes.

Haleema gently places Yusuf in my lap as she scurries away into the kitchen. My entire family surrounds me in a sparkling house I built. We all sit on the floor, our knees against our chest or crossed in our laps. Being able to hold my son, see my wife smile, and sit among my blood and my family fills me with an indescribable sense of pride and happiness.

My father enters the room. He had gone to the mosque to pray a nafal shukrana—prayer for gratitude—for my return. My cousins move out of their way for him. He sits behind me on a chair as I sit on the ground leaning into his knees with my arms on his lap and Yusuf in my lap.

Siraj draws nearing to me as he pinches Yusuf's cheeks. Thick black hair covers Siraj's face.

"Bhaijaan, are you happy now?" I hear my aunt ask Papa.

"Here I am, sitting in a room filled with my siblings, their children, and grandkids. What more could make me happier?" he says while pointing his finger around the room.

Haleema enters the room with a red and black printed tablecloth. She spreads it out with the help of the other girls in the room, each person grabbing one of the four corners. My mother follows closely behind her, carrying a tray brimming with plates and glasses. It's a sight I've never witnessed in our humble home before; there are enough plates and glasses for everyone present to have their own.

Yusuf whines as he catches sight of Haleema. She swiftly takes him out of my lap and returns to the kitchen to bring the food.

They fill the tablecloth one by one with an array of dishes. Biryani, tikkah, daal, chhole, naan, samosa, nihari, karahi, and much more lay before us. The table boasts a variety of meats, including lamb, beef, goat, and chicken. It's a rare treat, as meat is only for special occasions.

The room fills with the mouthwatering aroma of home-cooked delights. It feels like a holiday, with the space illuminated by abundant food. The fragrant spices float in the air, teasing our senses.

With our sleeves rolled up, we eagerly dive into the feast. Papa takes the lead, filling my plate with orange and white grains of rice from the biryani. He then drizzles a tangy yogurt sauce over the rice. In return, I place a chicken tikka on his plate. We engage in a playful race, piling each other's plates with the dishes we know the other enjoys.

As I take my first bite, a heavenly sensation floods my mouth. The harmonious blend of various flavors dances on my tongue. Even the taste of the tomatoes and yogurt seems more satisfying. Nothing I or the men I live within Cambridge can create compares to the taste of my mother's hands. Her cooking ability is an art—the flavor stored in her hands.

My head dips slightly, my belly content and my heart full. I try to capture the memory in my head. If only I had a bottle to capture the emotions in this room.

A sense of peace settles in my heart, knowing that over these past months, my family has been well-fed and able to improve our home.

"Raja, you must be tired," my father says. "Haleema, take him inside and get him in bed."

"Yes, Papa," Haleema obeys.

"Yusuf is usually asleep by now too. Don't worry about anyone still here," Papa says as we head toward our room.

Once in my room, I change out of my clothes and collapse onto the bed. Haleema joins me after putting Yusuf to sleep. It's been so long I am not sure how to touch her and what she'll be comfortable with. It's been months, years since I have felt her beautiful body.

My fingers trace her body, rubbing her skin against my palms. I'm hesitant, unused to the way it feels. I craved her skin and taste for months. She feels different, and my hands tremble as if I am feeling her for the first time.

"Every second you were gone felt like years passing by," Haleema whispers.

"I..." I don't know where to start. I want to tell her how I yearned for her, her voice, and her mind. I want to tell her I am never leaving her again.

"You are my entire heart, Haleema. You are the reason I breathe, the air within my lungs," I whisper in her ear. My lips tickle her ear as I inch closer. I push the hair away from her face and rub my nose against her soft cheeks. She smiles, covering her teeth with her hand. We are leaning into each other slowly once again.

"Haleema, when the wedding festivities are over, I am taking you back with me," I say.

She holds my face. Rubs my forehead and kisses my nose.

"Whatever you want, jaan," she says with a smile.

I hold her close and feel our hearts beat at the same pace. I want to tell my heart to hush down. People are sitting in the living room. They will hear. I pull her closer to me gently, never wanting to let go. She moves closer to me and rests her head against my chest. Her gold bangles cling together as she moves her hands up and down my arm.

I push her hair aside and kiss her slender neck softly. She breathes heavily. I stop, not wanting to rush things. It's been a while, and I want her to be comfortable with me. I lie back down and play with her hair, loving every bit and inch of her, every essence. I am back now, and I will return with her.

Through our window, the moonlight peers in. The light dances against Haleema's doting face. I am enchanted, never having witnessed anyone nearly as beautiful.

* * *

The next night, music pierces through my ears. My feet feel the sound of the speakers vibrating the floor. It is the night of my sister's wedding, and I made it just in time.

A man approaches me with a full beard and a child in his arms. He is wearing an adjrak shawl with tiny mirrors sticking on it with maroon and black embroidery around the edges. He lifts his hand to shake mine. As he greets me, I realize it's Aziz.

"You recognize me?" Aziz asks with a smile.

"Of course, Aziz. How could I have forgotten about you?" I rub his shoulder as I say it.

"How's America?" Aziz says.

"It was good. I have a business there, and I need to keep it running," I lie. Not sure why. But I don't want him to think less of me.

"I started a business shortly after you left," Aziz says. My eyes widen in shock.

"After you left the zoo, Salim bhai started getting more bird shipments and expanded his land further. I would spend every day looking after the animals and save up enough money to buy my own plot of land. Now I sell goats, cows, and chickens to meat shops." As Aziz speaks, a pregnant woman with a baby in her arms walks over.

"This is my wife and my child," Aziz says, pointing to the woman and her stomach. The woman greets me while looking at the ground and not making eye contact out of respect.

"Sometimes I wonder if I had gotten on that ship like you, I would be living life in America," Aziz says as another guest talks to him. I overhear the other guest at the wedding congratulating Aziz on the new house he had just bought in the neighborhood.

My eyes fixate on Aziz. He stayed here and now is about to be a father again and has bought a piece of land where he sells animals and makes a lucrative enough profit that he has purchased a house in a nice neighborhood. When I met him, he had barely enough money to buy a new pair of shoes. Now, he has enough to provide for a family in a new home. If I had stayed, would I have been able to provide for my family just the same? My stomach burns, and my throat hardens as envy washes over me.

I could have my own company and watch Yusuf grow. But Aziz gets to raise his family and still works with animals and is making more now. Would my life have been this way if I stayed?

"You are taking Haleema back with you?" Aziz asks. I had not mentioned it to others yet, but my intention for coming back was to bring Haleema and my son back with me.

"I hope to bring her back. Once all the wedding days are over. I'll get her visa now that I have a green card," I say.

"That's wonderful. How did you get a green card?" Aziz curiously asks.

"Oh, it's a long process. Hey, Aziz. I have to check on my parents. It was nice to see you. Remember me in your prayers," I say, trying to avoid the conversation and return to my family.

The music is still booming, and the party is going on. It has been years since I have been to an event like this. Nothing like this exists for me in the foreign lands I am escaping, yet I wish I were back. Everything feels different about home. People have more children that I don't know how to interact with. The city smells different, and the sounds of rickshaws alarm me at first.

I scan for Haleema in the crowd. She is wearing a beautiful yellow outfit, covered in jewels from head to toe. She looks elegant enough to be the bride herself. When we got married, I didn't have enough money to make sure she looked pampered this way. But now, seeing her this way makes my heart melt.

"Your beauty is tormenting me," I whisper in her ear, making her blush. Her cheeks turn a bright ruby rose. The public display of affection always makes her uncomfortable, reminding me of the days when I would wait for hours in her neighborhood or after her school just to glimpse her beauty.

"Can you hold Yusuf for a bit?" She hands me our son. He wails, still not knowing who I am and wanting more comfort in the crowds of people at the wedding.

The party continues as people sing and dance together. My sister makes her way down to the stage, her hands covered in henna. People approach the stage to feed her milky sweets.

The noise and all the people approaching overwhelm me. This never bothered me before, but I got used to the quiet life.

Haleema and I leave the party early and head to bed. While in bed, I think about how much things have changed at home. How I have changed and what I grew up with now feels foreign.

The following day, I ask Haleema to get ready and take her to the immigration office. I want to start the paperwork and get her visa as soon as possible.

We hop into a rickshaw, so overused that the seat covers are coming off. In America, all the taxi seats are well-kept. Things like this don't exist.

When we arrive at the immigration office, I pull out my green card and explain that I am here to get my wife a visit visa to the United States and when I get her to America, I will convert it to a green card. I speak in English only to show that I have been in Cambridge for a long time.

The office doesn't ask any questions. I find it odd that he is not speculating or trying to learn more about our situation. Maybe he sees the two-year-old, a young couple, and my green card and understands what is happening.

"Leave your passports here and come back tomorrow to pick them up. We will try to process your visa." Excitement fills my body. That's it! That's all I had to say and do to get the visa.

"Oh, thank you. Thank you," I shout. Before he can change his mind, we leave our passports behind and leave the office.

While waiting for another rickshaw, Haleema seems gloomy. She hunches over in her seat with her arms crossed.

"What's wrong?" I ask her.

"Nothing is wrong," she says, brushing her hair out of her face. "I went to the same office with Yusuf in my arms, pleading to get a visit visa to see you. They never believed me. I'm just frustrated by them, and I will miss it here. Our home is here. Our people are here. We are going to go live a life in foreign lands when we could be happy here. We can stay here," Haleema says.

"But life is much better there. If I didn't leave, you would have never been able to wear those clothes last night. The party wouldn't have been that lavish," I try to explain to her. She doesn't know what she is talking about.

I don't want to stay here longer than I need to. I used to be up all night thinking about my home; now that I am here, things feel different. Everything around me is different. Haleema and I will get to start a new life together.

CHAPTER 22

PHONE CARD

—

September 30, 1991

The past year with Haleema has rendered my spirit. Her first winter was brutal to acclimatize to, and I would have to remind her daily to cover her head with a wool hat and wear wool socks.

Haleema and I live in our tiny one-bedroom apartment in a brick building in Arlington. The house is nothing like where I lived with Saife on Chauncy Street. This one has only two rooms, with one of our bedrooms filled with Haleema's clothes and pictures from our wedding and another room with the sofas covered in floral print fabric sown by Haleema. The sofas match the green and dark magenta floral print curtains Haleema sewed.

We are minutes away from the preschool that Yusuf attends. Haleema bundles our son up in the winter and walks him to school in front of Spy Pond. His teacher, Ms. DeRosa, is a lovely woman dressed in dinosaurs, crayons, or alphabet-printed A-line dresses.

"Listen, I've been thinking about something," Haleema says as she rests her hand on the mound of her stomach. She rubs the bump gently. We are expecting another baby in a few months.

"What is it, dear?" I ask her.

"Whatever happened to those animals you were supposed to bring?" she asks. I stop tearing out checks and look up at her. We are silent. The only sound we hear is the TV playing in the other room as Yusuf listens to nursery rhymes.

"I'm not sure," my voice trails off.

"Did anyone ever find them anywhere? Did Saleem bhai ever ask you?" she ponders. Her bold dark eyes stare into my eyes. She brushes away the stray hairs tickling her face while waiting for my response.

"I don't think they ever showed up," I say, readjusting my glasses that keep slipping down my nose as I look down at the checkbook before me.

"I remember speaking to Saleem bhai, and I can't remember our conversation. There are many risks in his business of sending animals across the world. Sometimes the animals don't make it to their destination. And sometimes, like for me, only one animal makes it."

"Like that gray parrot?" Haleema points at the cage. I was thinking about myself, but she is right. Two animals made it off that boat—the gray parrot and me.

"Yes, like that parrot," I say while admiring the parrot. Saife had taken care of the parrot while I was in Karachi.

I walk over to the cage to check if I refilled her food this morning. Haleema stays seated on the sofa with a novel in her lap. She plays with the end of her braid as she flips through the pages. A few white strands show in her hair now. They shine against her dark black hair of hers.

"Did you try looking for them?" she asks after a pause of silence.

"I looked everywhere I could. I sometimes think the animals brought me here for a better life rather than me bringing them here," I say.

Yusuf comes running into the room with a mischievous smile on his face. "Park?" he asks.

"No, Mama took you yesterday," Haleema responds, shaking her head.

"I can take him," I say, bouncing off the sofa. "Let's go to the park!" I tell him. Yusuf grabs his light-up sneakers and rushes toward Haleema to put them on.

We walk to the park as Yusuf's shoes light up with every step he takes. Yusuf mainly likes to play in the sandbox or on the swings at the park. He quickly gets tired of the swings and doesn't want to push himself.

As the sun is about to set, the clouds turn a light pink and lilac in the sky.

"Come on, Yusuf. Mama misses us. It's time to go home," I call out to him in the sandbox.

He rushes over to his bike and pedals a few feet. "Papa, I tired. Pick me?" he asks, stretching out his hands.

"Of course, my child," I say, picking him up.

As I carry Yusuf in my arms, I think about what Haleema might have made for dinner. The way she cooks brings me home. It feels like I am back with my family, eating a warm spicy meal of lentils and rice.

We arrive home, and I see my reflection in the glass door. This time I am carrying a badge of honor, my son. We buzz the door open, and Haleema lets us inside. As we make our way up the stairs, I hear our door prop open. Haleema must have missed Yusuf. She always loves running after him in the park or seeing him smile while swinging.

As I walk to our apartment, I spot Haleema standing in the doorway. Tears are running down her face as she covers her mouth. My knees weaken, and I place Yusuf on the floor.

"What happened, Haleema?" I say as I rush up the stairs.

"Jahangir," she says, my name for the first time. My heart beats hard. She takes Yusuf from me.

"What happened?" I ask again, leaning into her to hold her. I know she wasn't feeling well. Is our baby okay?

She sobs as she rests her head on my chest. There is no smell of food, and the table isn't set.

I hold her close to me. "Haleema, everything will be okay. Just tell me what happened." I kiss the top of her head and brush her hair away from her face.

"Papa," I hear her say. My heart sinks into my throat.

"What happened to your father?" I ask her.

"No," Haleema responds. She sobs harder, trying to catch her breath. The black kohl in her eyes spread across her face. I wipe away her tears and gently kiss her on the top of her head.

"Papa had another stroke," As the words leave her mouth, I hold my breath.

"And…" Haleema says in between catching her breath. "He's no longer with us." This can't be true. I must have heard her wrong. My brain fogs up. I can't think anymore.

We had just bought our tickets to visit during Yusuf's winter break, which is only three months away.

"They said they will wait for you to come for the namaz-e-janaza," Haleema utters. She yanks at the scarf around her neck and wipes her tears.

"No, this can't be true," I utter in disbelief. "I didn't get to buy him a new flat in Karachi, one with a nice ocean view." I choke on my words while Haleema holds my hand. Her soft skin rubs my hand gently.

"Haleema," I say. "I didn't get to do enough for him. I didn't get to say goodbye." I freeze. Unable to move, unable to think, unable to react.

"You did more for him than you ever imagined," she says as she rests her head on my chest. "Do you want to call your mother?"

I do not have the courage or strength to talk to my mother. What agony she must be going through.

"We have a phone card left. I can dial the numbers," she says.

Haleema holds my face in both of her hands. She leaves the room and reappears with a small plastic rectangular card in her hand. She grabs the black phone and spins it a few times to untangle the spiral cord. She holds the phone to her ear. I hear the muffled sounds of an operator.

"Hello," Haleema says.

"Asalam Alaykum, Mama," I hear Haleema say as she holds back her tears. "Yes, he is home now. Do you want me to give him the phone?" Haleema slowly hands me the phone.

I put the phone near my ear. "Hello," I whisper.

"Raja, my beloved child," she says softly. "Your Papa is in a much better place. Looking down at us from heaven. Truth is, Raja, my child, your Papa was not doing well for six months. We hid this from you. We did not want you to worry. You are going to come in just a few months. We didn't want you to worry from another world away." Mama sniffs between words.

Papa was sick, and no one told me. I could have come back to take care of him. I could have sent him to the best hospital in Karachi. I could have sent more money for his treatment or medicine from here. My blood boils. Why didn't anyone tell me? I could have kept my father alive for a few months. At least I could have seen him.

My mother waits for me to say something.

"Raja, it's okay. We can't live forever," Mama says, sniffling harder on the phone.

"I am going to get on a flight tomorrow," I finally say.

"No, my child. We are not going to wait to bury him. His soul must rest. You, Haleema, Yusuf, and the new baby should come all together in a few months. You can't leave Haleema in this condition alone," she reassures me. "After all, we can't bring him back. He is gone."

"You have ten minutes left," the operator announces through the phone.

"Child, talk to your brothers. Remember your father in your prayers. He was in much pain after his first stroke, and it only worsened. He is out of the pain and suffering now. Allah hafiz, my dearest child," she says as I hear her hand the phone to someone else.

I hand the phone to Haleema and let her use up the remaining ten minutes. She talks into the telephone while rubbing my back, consoling me.

My eyes peer over to the corner of our living room where two leather suitcases stand, propped up on their wheels. In front of the suitcases is a VCR set in a cardboard box. In them are button-down shirts wrapped in clear plastic for my brothers and two brown and pink leather handbags for my sisters. I wanted Papa to open the VCR box I bought. He was going to be the first one to use it. I wanted him to see how many gifts I brought back. I was going to get him every candy to try.

"Allah hafiz," Haleema repeatedly says on the phone before placing it down in its place.

She looks over at me with her weary eyes, silently asking if I am okay. I look away and hold my face in my hands as she wraps her arms around me.

Yusuf comes running into the room with his new light-up toy sword. It makes hitting noises as he shakes it.

"He was in immense pain, my love," Haleema says. Her slender fingers gently glide through my hair, offering a tender touch of comfort. Drawing me closer, her heart beats fast and her body is warm. With a heavy heart, I rest my head upon her gentle, comforting mound of a stomach. Tears cascade down my face, and each breath becomes an arduous struggle. As my tears flow uncontrollably, I stifle my sobs and press my hand against my mouth, the anguish overwhelming my chest.

"He is so proud of you," she says as she rubs my face. I feel our baby inside her kick. Even our baby is trying to console me.

"I just didn't get to do enough for him," I say.

"What would have ever been enough? You fixed the entire house while being away; all he ever wanted was for you to be there. He would have traded the house for you instead," she says. "You would have bought him a new house, and then you would think a mansion would be better. Then you'd buy him a mansion, and you'd think an estate would be better, and then you'd buy him an estate and think buying him a city would be better," she says as she lifts my face off her stomach.

I wipe away my tears and sit up on the sofa. I can see my tears on Haleema's red and white flower-printed outfits. The hem of her shirt is laced with matching red and silver ribbon. She takes the end of her shift and wipes my face.

"Nothing will ever feel enough in your heart. That's because Allah gave you the biggest one, enough to house everyone in the world in it." She holds my face in both hands and slowly leans in to embrace me. Her hair smells like mustard oil.

Nothing I ever did for Papa would ever be enough for me. Haleema embraces me in her tender arms and rubs my back. Her affection nurtures me. I feel like a child, weak in her arms. I am frail and unable to move. She consoles me while carrying our baby in her.

ACKNOWLEDGMENTS

Writing a book is never alone. Many people are involved in bringing a novel to fruition.

Thank you to my loved ones for never letting me give up throughout the writing process. Thank you to my parents, Syed Rehman and Haleema Rehman, for raising me in a humble household with an infinite supply of love and affection. Thank you to my siblings and cousins, Jahangir Rehman, Farzeen Rehman, Saife Rehman, Takreem Zulfiqar, Fareen Fareed, Mohammad Fahad, Waheed Syed, Mohammad Ali, Shadi Al Hindi, Mujtaba Ali, and Amari Powell for always being my oasis in a desert, a source of nurture, as I struggled to complete this book.

Thank you to Eric Koester, Cassandra Caswell-Stirling, Chrissy Wolfe, and everyone at Manuscripts LLC for your guidance throughout the program. Thank you to the Summer 2022 cohort for all the support!

I would never have finished this book without my incredible friends who read and edited many drafts. Thank you to Jenna Caldwell for brushing a little of your golden dust of talent and generosity onto me. Thank you to Jillian Castoro, who answered my late-night calls as anxiety filled my heart.

Thank you to Sophia Lockwood for your wisdom and support. Also, thank you to Shubhan Nagendra for the emotional support and for reading my book several times over to provide your thoughtful feedback. I am indebted to you all. And thank you to everyone who supported *The Zookeeper* when it was only a dream. I asked you all for your support when my book was barely a manuscript. I would not have been able to publish this book without the following:

Sohaib Abbasi, Saphia Abouelenein, Zainab Adisa, Awais Ahmad, Azeem Ahmed, Tahreem Akhtar, Shadi Al Hindi, Mujtaba Ali, Jessica Almazan, Rosella Aluia, Natasha Anis, Elizabeth Beaton, Millicent Bender, Kelly Benoit, Janika Berridge, Andrea Brenner, Noah Brown, Darcie Brown, Marcy Campos, Sarah Chamberlain, Janice Chan, Tanvi Chopra, Andrew Clarke, Alex Crowley, Jenna Crutcher, Denali Dahl, Gaurav Dangol, Phillip Davis, Martin DeLuca, Rachel Domond, Sol Durrani, Jimmy Ellis, Shannon Exley, Mohammad Fahad, Fareed Fareed, Mohammad Farhan, Lucy Faust, Talia Flores, Genesis Fuentes, Nimisha Ganesh, Harry Gilliard, Sarah Glover, Priyanka Gulati, Said Haji, Nerses Haroutunian, James Helou, Usma Hosain, Mohammed Irfan, Conor Jackman, Rafay Jafri, Adnan Kabir, Elizabeth Kamya, Subandha Karmacharya, Julia Kerr, Mahnoor Khalid, Tehreem Khan, Ahmer Khan, Zehra Khan, Danish Khan, Talha Kidwai, Richard Kiker, Adrienne Klein, Daniel Knoll, Nathan Kumar, Aseem Kumar, Maria Lobo, Alexander Lopez-Perez, Jeta Luboteni, Hana Manadath, Jennifer Martinez, Dan Matlack, Mike McCabe, Jaime McCarthy, Jean Mejia, Tano Mejia, Maddy Mele, Joseph Janik Miller, Kim Miller, Taameen Mohammad, Stephanie Montaño, Mallory Mrozinski, Rabia Muhammad, Abina Nepal, Emma Niden, Maha Noor, Yuta Otake, Yazmin Padilla, Satinder

Parmar, Dan Perry, Patricia Peruta, Shannon Pinzon, Amari Powell, Ammad Quraishi, Maria Qureshi, Shreyas Ravinshankar, Miles Robinson, Fanon X Rogers, Ariela Rose, Victoria Rose, Kenya Roy, Meriam Salem, Solomon Self, Nicole Sener, Syed Shah, Olivia Shalhoup, Asim Shamim, Roshni Sharma, Aisha Siddqi, Sumbul Siddiqui, Ivan Solomon, Tessa Sontheimer, Lucy Srour, Izzi Stern, Emma Stewart, Mustafa Sunka, Haniya Syeda, Sobia Syeda, Shanze Tahir, Barry Thrasher, Sidi Traore, Kenta Utsunomiya, Sophia Celeste Vos Garfi, Snowdon Vose, Kiran Waqar, Emily Watkins, Jenny Weaver, David Weinstein, Teanna Willis, Keith Witham, and Sumaiya Zama.

Lastly, I want to acknowledge myself for accomplishing something I've always wanted yet feared.